C

It is not very easy to help two entirely different people away from their homes at the same time, but that is what eleven-year-old Ben Mallory had to do when, during his stay with his father and stepmother-to-be in London, he went off exploring on his own and made two unexpected friends, who couldn't, he suddenly realized, be left to fend for themselves.

Not content with evading the dangerous political enemies of Thomas's father (who was an exiled East African Prime Minister), Ben found himself saddled with nine-year-old Lil as well, who was on the run from 'The Welfare', who were determined to take her in hand while her mother was in hospital.

Sometimes their forced escape was exciting, sometimes so dangerous that Ben thought longingly of Aunt Mabel's cosy house that was his home and of her brisk voice telling him to do his homework. But he had to go on, had even to give up his dearest possession at the pawn-shop so that they could buy food, had to find somewhere safe for them to hide, climb an impossible cliff face, and outwit their enemy 'Baldy'. For gentle Thomas showed courage, and Lil, who was only a girl, and an irritating one at times, had more brains than he liked to admit and was fierce in her loyalty.

Altogether things were never quite what you might expect, Ben found, and he emerged from their adventure triumphant – but also wiser and braver if not at all sadder.

This is an adventure story that is all the more exciting because it could really have happened. For all readers of ten to thirteen.

NINA BAWDEN

ON THE RUN

PUFFIN BOOKS

Puffin Books, Penguin Books Ltd, Harmondsworth, Middlesex, England
Penguin Books, 625 Madison Avenue, New York, New York 10022, U.S.A.
Penguin Books Australia Ltd, Ringwood, Victoria, Australia
Penguin Books Canada Ltd, 2801 John Street, Markham, Ontario, Canada L3R 1B4
Penguin Books (N.Z.) Ltd, 182–190 Wairau Road, Auckland 10, New Zealand

—

First published by Victor Gollancz 1964
Published in Puffin Books 1967
Reprinted 1972, 1974, 1975, 1976, 1977, 1978, 1980, 1982, 1983

—

—

Made and printed in Great Britain
by Hazell Watson & Viney Ltd,
Aylesbury, Bucks
Set in Monotype Bembo

CONTENTS

I

THE WALL

THERE are two things to remember about adventures. They always happen when you are not expecting anything to happen and the beginning is usually quite unexciting and ordinary so that you seldom realize that something important has begun. Adventure always creeps up on you from behind.

Certainly Ben's adventure did. It started on a hot, windless day in late summer; the sort of day that is only comfortable if you are swimming in the sea. But Ben was nowhere near the sea. He was sitting, feeling sticky and bored, in a small flat in London, near the Zoo. Because he was bored he had just eaten eight honey and sultana sandwiches, six chocolate biscuits, and three cream cakes. He was wondering with half his mind if he could possibly manage another cream cake without being sick, when his father said,

'Why don't you go and play in the garden, old chap?'

Though Ben had been thinking of doing just that – with the half of his mind that wasn't wondering about the next cream cake – the fact that his father had suggested the garden turned him against it at once. He wasn't often contrary but he was feeling heavy and cross and he knew his father wanted to get rid of him so that he could sit on the sofa with Miss Shirley Mackingtosh and hold her hand, in private.

'Nothing to do in the garden,' he said. This wasn't true, Ben was a resourceful person who could find something to do in an empty yard, but he knew his father would think it was. The flat was at the top of a tall, thin house in a terrace of tall, thin houses. The garden was like all the other gardens in the row: a small oblong bounded on three sides by high, yellow

walls and dark as the bottom of a well. It smelt like a well:
dank and mossy. Nothing grew except a plane tree and a few
nasturtiums, struggling on weak, white stems up towards the
sunlight that never penetrated there. Nobody played there
either, except Ben sometimes and the cats who knocked the
lids off the dustbins at night.

'I suppose there isn't much to do,' Ben's father said. He
glanced at Miss Mackingtosh and gave a little sigh. She smiled
back at him and said, to Ben, 'I'm afraid you're finding London rather a dull place, aren't you?'

Ben was ashamed. It was ungrateful to be bored when they
had tried so hard to amuse him. 'Not really. I mean there's all
sorts of places to go, like the Tower and the Planetarium and
... and the place with all the pictures you took me to
yesterday.'

'The National Gallery. Did you enjoy that, Ben? I wasn't
sure whether it was the sort of place to take a wee laddie.'

'I enjoyed it very much,' Ben said quickly, smiling at her
and thinking how pretty she was and wishing she wouldn't
call him a wee laddie in that put-on Scottish voice and that he
knew what to call *her*. He couldn't say 'you' all the time.
Shirley? Some grown-ups didn't like children calling them by
their christian names. Aunt Shirley? She wasn't his aunt. Miss
Mackingtosh? That had been all right when he first met her,
but it seemed rather cold and stand-offish now.

The reason Ben was in this quandary was that next week
Miss Mackingtosh was going to marry his father, who was a
widower. Ben's mother had died four years ago and since then
he had lived with his brother and sister, John and Mary, and
their Aunt Mabel, in a town called Henstable, by the sea.
Their father, who was working for an insurance company,
lived alone in his flat in London and Aunt Mabel said it was
a good thing he was marrying again because now he would
have someone to cook good meals for him and look after him
properly. But although John and Mary and Ben had tried hard

to be glad for their father's sake, they still felt very strange about it and were shy of Miss Mackingtosh who was also shy of them. It was Aunt Mabel who had suggested they went to stay with their father, one at a time.

'It's easier to get along with people when you're on your own with them,' she had said. 'And the three of you together – well, you just scare her.'

'What do we do wrong?' Ben asked indignantly. 'We're ever so quiet and polite. We don't bounce at her or shout or anything.'

Aunt Mabel sighed. 'No. You just sit on the sofa, all three of you, and stare at her as if she had green hair and a third eye in the middle of her forehead. Poor girl.'

'She's not a girl. She's pretty old.'

'Thirty-six,' Aunt Mabel said. 'I daresay she still has some of her faculties ... Though whether she will have, after a whole week of you ...' She looked at Ben and added, in a different tone, 'Be good, won't you? Not just because she's going to be your stepmother, but because she's a shy person who would like to be friends if you'd let her.'

'I don't even know what to call her,' Ben said miserably. 'I can't call her Stepmother. They're always horrible and she's ...'

'There aren't any rules,' Aunt Mabel said. 'You'll have to work it out between you.'

She put on her this-is-none-of-my-business-and-I'm-not-going-to-interfere expression and Ben remembered something John had said. *I expect once they're married we'll have to go and live with Dad and HER. We'll have to leave Aunt Mabel's and go and live in London.*

'I don't want to go,' Ben said suddenly and passionately. 'I want to stay here with you.' He flung himself at Aunt Mabel and hid his face in her flat chest. 'I don't like London. It's dirty and smelly. And why have *I* got to go? Why not John or Mary? It's not fair. I'm the youngest.'

'Just because,' Aunt Mabel said mysteriously. Then she rumpled Ben's hair and said, 'Get on with you, what a *fuss*. Good heavens, boy, it's only for a week . . .'

The trouble was that now it was going to be much longer than a week. Aunt Mabel had written to say John and Mary had measles and, as Ben had not been in contact with them, he ought not to come home until they were better.

This had depressed Ben. Although his father and Miss Mackingtosh had been kind to him, what he had told Aunt Mabel was true: he didn't like London, especially not in this dreadful heat wave. Even if you climbed to the top of Primrose Hill as they had done this morning, there was hardly any breeze. The trees were so still they might have been painted on the background of grey buildings that shimmered in the misty heat. How different the air felt at Henstable, Ben thought; lovely and clean and gusty. Here it was so warm and sluggish he could hardly breathe.

He went over to the open window. He could see Regent's Park and the front of the Zoo. He thought of the lions in their concrete and iron cages.

'The lions must be so *hot*,' he said, putting his hand out of the window to see if it was cooler outside.

'It's much hotter in Africa,' his father reminded him. 'Don't you remember, when you first came to England you said it was so cold that you thought you would shrivel up and die.'

'That was years and years ago,' Ben said. 'My blood has thickened up since, Aunt Mabel says. I'm a cold climate person now.'

It seemed odd, he thought, that he should have forgotten how hot it was in Africa. He had been born there and lived there until he was seven. Now he was nearly twelve and when he tried to remember about that time it seemed to slip away from him like something that had happened in a dream. All he could remember clearly was his best friend, Thomas, and his pet chameleon, Balthazar . . .

He said, 'Perhaps people are like chameleons. What they're like depends on the place they live in. I'm a Henstable person now, though perhaps if I lived in London, I'd change.'

'That's a clever idea, Ben,' Miss Mackingtosh said – rather foolishly, Ben thought. As if she expected him to be too young to have ideas at all.

His father said, 'I'm sorry you're stuck here in this heat, but we couldn't send you back to catch measles, could we?'

He sounded cheerful enough but there was a slightly sad look on his face. Almost, Ben thought, *almost* as if his father wished he *could* send him back.

This gave Ben a queer feeling. He had been a bit grumpy today perhaps, because today was the day he should have gone home to Henstable, but he hadn't been rude or behaved really badly, had he? He looked at his father nervously.

Then he realized what was wrong. It was nothing he had done. That was a relief, of course, but it also meant there was nothing he could do to put it right. His father was just as upset by Aunt Mabel's letter as he had been, because if Ben had to stay in London, then his father had to stay too, to look after him. And that meant that when he got married next week, he and Miss Mackingtosh wouldn't be able to go to Ireland for their honeymoon as they had arranged to do.

'I don't mind getting measles,' Ben blurted out at once. 'I've got to get it sometime, haven't I?'

'I wasn't thinking of you,' his father said in a rather tart voice. 'I was thinking of Mabel. She's got enough, with two invalids in the house already.'

Ben saw by the hurt expression on his father's face that he hadn't understood him. He had just thought that Ben had been so unhappy in the flat that he would rather catch measles than stay any longer.

He said, 'I only meant – I meant, I'm a bother to you. About

the wedding and the honeymoon. But it's all right. I mean –
I'll be all right. I don't mind staying here by myself.' As he
thought about it, it seemed a splendid idea. 'I can cook bacon,'
he said, 'and make tea and look after the flat for you and . . .'

His voice trailed away. He could see the broad, affectionate
grin spreading over his father's face.

He said, 'That's very nice of you, Ben. Very thoughtful.
But of course you can't look after yourself. And it doesn't
matter.' He smiled at Miss Mackingtosh. 'We can easily put
off our holiday, can't we, Shirley dear?'

Miss Mackingtosh smiled back, but it was rather a little
smile and Ben could tell that even if his father didn't mind,
she did.

This made him miserable. Though he sometimes thought she
was silly – when she called him a wee laddie and said things
like 'I'm sure Someone would like a sweetie, wouldn't he?' –
he knew she tried to be kind and he didn't want to spoil her
honeymoon. But it seemed, all the same, that he *was* going to
spoil it and there was nothing he could do about it.

Nothing at all.

He gave a deep sigh, fetched right up from his boots, and
said, 'I think I'll go and play in the garden, if you don't mind.'

At least he could leave them alone to hold hands and kiss.
He wouldn't have minded their kissing while he was there,
but they didn't seem to want to. Whenever he came into the
room one of them always got up from the sofa where they
had been sitting together and moved to another chair.

Miss Mackingtosh said, 'If Someone looked in that carrier
bag by the window, he might find a nice, new tennis ball.'

'Thank you,' Ben said. He got the tennis ball. 'Thank you
very much.'

As he went out of the room he heard Miss Mackingtosh say,
'Isn't he *sweet*.'

'Sweet,' Ben said to himself disgustedly as he walked down
the narrow stairs to the back door. '*Sweet*. My God!'

Outside the door, he stood on the steps that led down into the dank garden and considered what to do.

He could go to the Zoo. He had enough pocket-money left. But he didn't really enjoy the Zoo. He had been twice already this week, once with his father and once with Miss Mackingtosh who had stood for hours outside the monkey cage, watching the monkeys pick fleas out of each other. She kept saying, 'Look, Ben, aren't they sweet?' Ben had soon tired of the monkeys. He was really only interested in the lions and once he had looked at them there was no point in looking at them again. They didn't do anything; just lay in their cages and looked incredibly weary and bored.

Ben was sorry for them. Once, in Africa, he had seen a pride of lions stalking a hartebeest. It was the lionesses who did the work, as they always did. The lion just lay in the shadow of a big rock, grand and lazy as an old king. His wives stole up behind the hartebeest who was unwisely grazing too far from his herd. They moved slowly, in single file, lying down whenever the hartebeest looked up. They looked rather as if they were playing a game of Grandmother's Footsteps.

Watching from the car, Ben had felt curiously divided. He wanted them to catch the hartebeest, but he wanted him to get away too. It was a strange feeling and it had made him feel slightly sick. Then, after about half an hour of the Grandmother's Footsteps game, the hartebeest looked up. The leading lioness froze into a statue carved out of pale sandstone, but the hartebeest saw her. He blew out loudly and contemptuously through his nose, lifted up his heavy head and set off at a trot, moving rather slowly as if to show the lions that he wasn't really running away, he wasn't really frightened of them ... The lioness had stood up; she was too far away to kill so she stretched and yawned, pretending that she hadn't really been serious about it. She padded back to join the other lionesses and they had played for a while like big, tawny kittens in the fast falling African dusk.

Ben sighed. No, there was no point, while he could remember this, in going to look at lions in cages.

He walked slowly down to the bottom of the garden. The wall was high, but there were enough broken or missing bricks to make it an easy climb. From the top of the wall, you could look down into the other gardens. One or two had been tidied up with crazy paving and geraniums in tubs, but most were neglected and overgrown. The houses were old, the paint shabby and peeling, the brickwork dark with a hundred years of London soot. Every house had an iron fire-escape – a rusty stairway with a little platform here and there. On some of the platforms, people were sunning themselves in bathing costumes, lying in bright coloured deckchairs with their radios blaring beside them. The sun had turned most of them bright red, like boiled sweets.

No one took any notice of Ben. Even if the sun had not made them lazy, no one would have minded a boy trespassing on the wall at the end of their gardens. The houses were all divided into flats and so the gardens didn't belong to anyone in particular.

The top of the wall was about nine inches wide. It was easy to walk along but quite difficult to bounce a tennis ball while you were walking. Here and there the surface of the wall was jagged and broken, so it was important to aim the ball at a smooth part. As he moved along, Ben became more confident of his skill and bounced the ball higher and higher.

Suddenly the ball landed on a crumbly brick and shot forwards and sideways at an awkward angle. Ben lurched to catch it, missed, lost his balance and fell forward – not off the wall, but on to it, so that he ended crouched in an undignified position on hands and toes with his bottom sticking up in the air.

The whole of his stomach seemed to turn over. He was, for a moment, badly frightened. Not because he had so nearly fallen, but because the top of the wall just in front of him was

covered with jagged spikes of broken glass. The first spike –
a wicked piece that looked like the top of a broken bottle – was
only an inch away from his nose. If he had not been agile – or
lucky – he would have fallen right on top of it and cut his face
to pieces. He eased himself down carefully to sit astride the
wall and saw that the broken glass continued all round the
small garden that lay just in front of him, on his right side.
And his ball had bounced into it.

It had bounced – though of course he didn't realize it at the
time – straight into adventure.

2

THE PRISONER IN THE GARDEN

As soon as he had stopped being frightened, Ben began to
feel extremely indignant. People had no right to stick glass on
their walls where other people might want to walk and
bounce their balls.

'It's dangerous. Someone might get hurt.'

He spoke aloud, although he knew it was unlikely anyone
could hear him. The gardens were almost always empty and
this one – he could see a little of it if he leaned precariously
forward – was particularly desolate looking. There were shrubs
and a few stubby, disheartened trees, all overgrown with a
silvery tangle of old man's beard.

But there *was* someone there. Almost as soon as Ben had
spoken, a boy's head and shoulders appeared above the wall
a few yards away from Ben. He tossed the tennis ball towards
him.

Ben caught it and said, without thinking, '*Asanti sana.*'

Asanti sana means 'thank you very much' in Swahili. And

Ben had spoken in Swahili because the boy was African. He had a dark face with a purple sheen on it like a ripe plum and thick, black, woolly hair.

Not all Africans speak Swahili of course, but Ben hadn't had time to think of that. He hadn't thought at all, in fact. It was just that the boy's sudden appearance had shot him right back – back to the years before he came to England when he had helped his best friend, Thomas, mind his father's cows and talked in Swahili as easily and naturally as he talked in English.

This boy didn't look in the least like Thomas, though. It wasn't just that he was older than Thomas had been and much better dressed, in a very smart, white silk blouse. (Thomas had never worn anything except an old khaki shirt and sometimes a torn pair of khaki trousers.) Thomas had had a happy face that smiled most of the time but this boy looked sad in a strange grown-up way, like Aunt Mabel or Ben's father when they were worried about something.

He smiled, though in a stiff, shy way, and replied in Swahili.

Ben couldn't understand what he said and went red with shame and disappointment. 'I'm sorry – I can't – I mean, I've forgotten.'

The boy looked at him with his solemn dark eyes and repeated carefully, in English, 'Was that your ball? It fell on my head.'

'I didn't know you were there. I was just bouncing it.' Then Ben remembered why he had been frightened. He said heatedly, 'It's very dangerous to stick spikes of glass all over your walls. I might have cut myself and bled to death.'

'I'm sorry,' the boy said, sadly and politely. 'I didn't put the glass there.'

'Someone did though, didn't they? I mean it didn't just grow there. Your parents must have done, I suppose. Why are they so keen on keeping people out of your garden?'

The boy hesitated. 'It is not just to keep other people out. It is also to keep me *in*.'

'Whatever should they want to do that for?' Ben asked rudely. Then he caught his breath. 'Do you mean you are a sort of prisoner?'

Although this would be exciting, he didn't really believe it was likely. He remembered that when his brother John had been younger he was always making up stories in which he was a prisoner or a refugee or something. Once, he had gone around for a whole week in an old Trilby hat, pretending to be an escaped criminal in disguise. When Aunt Mabel took it away and burned it he was so upset that he refused to go out; he said the police were bound to catch him now. Aunt Mabel had given him a mighty dose of cascara. She said John had too much imagination and this was the only cure she knew.

Ben wondered if this boy was the same sort of person.

'I am not exactly a prisoner,' the boy said. 'But – but I am not allowed out alone. Last week I climbed out of the garden to visit a friend of mine. We went to the park. After that, they said I must never go out again without the detective and they sent for a workman to fix the glass on the walls . . .'

'What do you mean?' Ben's voice rose. 'Without a detective? That's a policeman . . .' He laughed loudly. Of course this boy was just like John. Whoever heard of a boy having a detective to take him out – like a nurse, or something.

The boy said nothing. Under the white blouse, his shoulders seemed to droop in a discouraged way.

Ben began to feel uncomfortable. Even if this boy was the most frightful liar, it was none of his business. He had no right to come along and bounce balls on his head and then be rude and disbelieving. He was beginning to wonder if he should apologize when the boy said, 'Why did you say thank you in Swahili?'

'I used to live in Africa when I was young. In Kenya.'

'What's your name?'

'Benjamin Mallory. What's yours?'

'Thomas Okapi.'

'I used to know a boy called Thomas,' Ben said. 'He was a Kikuyu.'

'Oh.' This Thomas looked over his shoulder in a nervous way as if he half expected someone to jump out from the bushes. Then he said, 'Why don't you – I mean, please will you come down?'

'How can I? Without cutting myself on your glass?'

'It is all right if you're careful. There is a place where I picked out some of the glass so that my friend could get in. And if I get off this ladder, you can come down it.'

'Who's your friend?'

'A girl. A girl who comes sometimes.'

Though Ben was careful, it wasn't easy. Even though he wriggled very slowly along the wall to the place Thomas had indicated, he still tore his trousers and cut his hand. Thomas looked at him anxiously as he jumped off the ladder.

'You're bleeding,' he said in a horrified voice.

'It'll stop in a minute,' Ben said carelessly. He felt gratified by the shocked expression on Thomas's face. 'I'm always cutting myself. It doesn't matter so long as you suck the poison out. How old are you?'

'Eleven.'

'I'm twelve,' Ben said, adding a month on to his age because now they stood on a level he could see that Thomas was taller than he was. But he was dressed in a very babyish way: in the white blouse, a pair of very short, blue linen trousers and long white socks, like a girl's. The socks and the shirt were very clean. Either he was made to change his clothes at least six times a day, Ben thought, or he never did anything to make himself dirty.

He said, feeling superior, 'Well, what shall we do now?'

'I don't know.' Thomas sounded uncertain. 'We – we could play with your ball.'

'There isn't enough room.' Ben looked round the garden. It was a very shut-in place, tangled and secret like a forgotten wood. The trees and bushes grew thickly; from where they stood they could not see the lower part of the house, only the roof and the chimneys that seemed to move against the sky.

'What do you usually do?' Ben asked, politely, remembering that he was a guest.

'I read books. And sometimes I am allowed to watch television if I have done my lessons properly.'

'I mean what do you do in the holidays,' Ben said impatiently. 'You don't do lessons in the holidays.'

'I don't have holidays.'

Ben stared at him. 'What do you mean? Everyone has holidays. When they're not at school.'

'I don't go to school,' Thomas said. He looked at Ben nervously as if he was afraid he would despise him for this. 'At home, in Africa, I have a tutor. Here, my uncle teaches me in the mornings. We do French and mathematics and history. And some afternoons Mr Baldry comes to teach me athletics. When he doesn't come, I have to play by myself. I have been building something in the garden. Come and look.'

He led Ben through the bushes to the other corner of the garden. In the angle of the walls, there was a rough sort of hut with low mud walls and a roof made out of plaited rush mats.

'It's like an African hut,' Ben said. 'Can you get inside?'

'I left a little hole for the door.'

They crawled inside. There was just room for the two of them. Enough light came through the door opening for Ben to see Thomas was looking at him expectantly.

He said, 'You've done it quite well. It's almost like a real African hut except that it's smaller, of course. And you ought to have a fire in the middle.' Things began to come back to him. He said dreamily, 'The smoke gets in your eyes and makes you cough and the chickens run in and out all the time.'

'I just pretend to have a fire and cook,' Thomas said shyly. 'It is not very well done, I'm afraid. The walls are too wet and slimy. The sun is not hot enough to dry the mud.'

'It's probably the wrong sort of earth, too,' Ben said kindly. He tried to think of something helpful. 'You should make patterns on the floor with dyes and things. Some huts are awfully pretty.'

'I've never been inside a real hut,' Thomas said.

Ben was surprised. 'I thought all Africans lived in huts.' He looked round and saw that against one wall was a pile of unopened tins – salmon, sardines and baked beans.

'I got those from the cook,' Thomas explained. 'I say they are for me, but they are really for Lil – that's my friend. She has an enormous appetite. She is always hungry.'

'Doesn't she get fed at home?' Ben asked. Normally it would not surprise him to hear someone was always hungry but at the moment he was feeling very full, after his tea, and he could not imagine anyone wanting to eat a tin of cold baked beans.

'I – I don't know,' Thomas said and then added quickly, as if he wanted to change the subject, 'Let's go outside. There is nothing to do in here.'

They crawled out and sat under the bushes. They looked at each other cautiously for a minute, then Thomas smiled and said, 'Would you like to see my ladybird?'

He took a small matchbox out of his pocket and Ben looked at a somewhat moribund ladybird. When he was small, he used to say, *Bishy, bishy, barney bee, Tell me when your wedding be*, but now he was too old for rhymes so he just touched the insect's wings experimentally. It lifted its spotted wings feebly, like a pair of tiny shutters, and let them fall again. 'I think it's almost dead,' Ben said.

20

Thomas closed the matchbox with a discouraged expression and Ben said hastily, 'I'll show you my penknife, if you like. And my horse.'

He took his two chief treasures out of his pocket along with a lump of hairy chewing gum and his collection of bus tickets. The penknife was a very good one John had given him on his last birthday; it had Ben's name on it and his address in Henstable. 'Careful, it's sharp,' he warned Thomas. 'It's got a saw and a tin-opener as well. And this is my horse, Pin.'

Pin was his tiny, cloudy-green, jade horse. He had pricked ears, delicate legs and a flying tail. 'My friend, Miss Pin, gave him to me for a keepsake,' Ben explained. 'He's very valuable.'

'He is beautiful,' Thomas said softly.

Ben put him back in his pocket. He was suddenly bored with sitting and talking. 'Let's have a wrestling match,' he suggested.

Thomas shook his head. 'I do not like fighting,' he said. He looked at Ben thoughtfully and added, 'Besides, it would be no fun. I know I should win.'

He spoke so simply – not boasting, just stating a fact – that it took Ben's breath away for a minute. When he had recovered he said in a low, dangerous voice, 'Oh, you do, do you?'

Thomas looked at him, as if puzzled. 'Yes,' he said, 'I . . .'

He stopped suddenly and sat back on his haunches, his head tilted to one side, listening. Suddenly, without understanding why, Ben knew he was frightened.

"What's the matter?' he whispered.

'I've got to go,' Thomas whispered back. 'She's . . .'

A woman's voice rang out across the garden. 'Thomas. Come here this minute.'

'Who is it?' Ben said, in an ordinary voice.

Thomas turned on him. 'Ssh – don't shout.'

'I wasn't shouting.'

'You were – she'll hear – she mustn't know.' Thomas's eyes

were wide and panicky. He said in a low, breathless voice, 'No one is supposed to come here. Stay where you are – don't move. *Please.*'

Thomas was so frightened that Ben began to be frightened himself.

'*Thomas,*' the woman called. Her voice grated, like someone running a nail over a blackboard.

'Coming,' Thomas answered. He stood up and pushed his way through the bushes.

For a second or two, Ben remained obediently still. Then curiosity got the better of him and he followed Thomas, moving slowly and cautiously in the direction of the woman's voice. Although the undergrowth was thick and concealing, the garden was really very small and the cover came to an end quite suddenly so that, creeping out from behind a bush, he found that he was now in full view of the house.

About twenty yards away, the width of a small, dried-up lawn, a woman was standing on the steps of the fire-escape. She was a stout woman in a dark blue dress. Her brown hair was scraped back from her face which was big and square, rather like a white shovel. She wasn't moving; only her eyes moved, very dark and glittering, as she watched Thomas come slowly up the steps of the fire-escape towards her.

Ben's heart gave a great jump up into his throat and he flung himself back behind the bush, flat on his stomach on the ground. He lay there, his face pressed into last year's dead leaves, his heart thumping. He wasn't sure why he was so afraid. She hadn't seen him – he was sure she hadn't seen him – but would it really have mattered so much if she had? After all, he wasn't a trespasser. Thomas had invited him into the garden. Why was Thomas afraid? Why was *he* afraid? Ben lifted his head cautiously, questions whirling round in his head. He heard the woman say, 'All right. Five minutes but no more. You know what will happen if you disobey me.'

Thomas's reply was inaudible. Ben craned his neck, peering

between two branches. He saw the woman go into the house through some french windows on the first floor and for a moment she stood there, quite still, looking out. Her face was white in the gloom. Ben had the horrible feeling that somehow she knew he was there . . .

Thomas was waiting by the hut. 'Where did you go? I told you to stay here.'

His voice was imperious – as if he were used to giving orders.

Ben was annoyed. 'Don't you speak to me like that,' he said. They glared at each other.

Then Thomas said humbly, 'I'm sorry. I did not mean to be rude. I was just afraid that Miss Fisher had seen you. She would be terribly angry.'

'Why?'

Thomas looked flustered. 'I – I can't explain now, it would take too long. I've got to go in.'

'You've got time to tell me why you're scared of her. Who is she?'

'The housekeeper. She looks after me. I'm not really scared of her but she is very strict. If I do not go in when she tells me, she locks me up as a punishment. The day Lil and I went to the park, she locked me up in the attic for the whole afternoon.'

Ben was deeply shocked. 'Why ever do you let her? I'd never let anyone do such a beastly thing to *me*.'

Thomas shrugged his shoulders. 'It wasn't beastly. Just boring. She only does it because she is afraid of what my uncles would say if anything should happen to me. I don't like her, but she is not *bad*. She would never betray me to my enemies.'

Ben wondered what Thomas could mean. Boys didn't have enemies, except in books. And yet Thomas had spoken so naturally, that it didn't sound like a story he was making up.

23

Ben said, 'She sounds absolutely horrible. If I had a person like that to look after me, I'd make a frightful fuss. Why don't you tell your mother?'

'My mother is in America with my younger brother.' Thomas looked suddenly sad. 'It is very lonely without him. We always played together. Please, Ben – please, will you come again tomorrow? I will leave the ladder for you and you can wait by the hut . . .'

'I might. I'll have to see,' Ben said off-handedly, though he was feeling very excited. He had just realized something. Surely, in England, the only people who had tutors, and detectives to watch over them were millionaires or royalty? Perhaps Thomas's father was a very rich man who was afraid Thomas would be kidnapped and held to ransom. Or perhaps he was an African Prince. But if he was a Prince, he wouldn't be frightened of Miss Fisher . . .

He said, 'Does your father know how she treats you, then?'

'No.'

'Is he in America, too?'

Thomas shook his head. 'He is in England.' His eyes were like pools of brown water with the sun shining on them. They looked at Ben in an unseeing, reflective way, as if he were turning something over in his mind.

Ben said, 'Well then – if he's here, why don't you just *tell* him?'

'I can't,' Thomas said in a low voice. 'He is in prison.'

'Oh,' Ben said. 'Oh.' He felt the blood rush up his neck and spread over his face. It was as if he were standing in front of a hot fire.

'I'm sorry,' he stammered. Oh – what a stupid idiot he was! What a *nit*. Why had he blundered on, asking questions like that? How awful Thomas must be feeling. Ben could hardly bear to look at him. He vowed silently that he would never, never ask anyone anything again.

But the very next second he said, 'What did he do?' He

couldn't help it; the words seemed to ooze out of him. He *had* to know.

'Do?' Thomas said. He sounded surprised. Ben felt even more ashamed.

'I only meant ...' he began, and was astonished to see Thomas smile.

'My father is not a criminal,' he said. 'He is not a thief or – or a murderer. He is a very good man.'

'But ...' Ben said, and stopped. He didn't understand, but he refused to ask any more questions.

Thomas was standing ramrod straight, his hands glued to his sides like a soldier on parade. He said, proudly, 'My father is a Prime Minister.'

3

A MATTER OF POLITICS

'DAD,' Ben said. 'Dad – do good people get put in prison?'

'Not often.' Mr Mallory was standing by Ben's bedroom door. He had just said good night and was about to switch off the light. Instead, he came and sat on the edge of Ben's bed. One of the nice things about him was that he always tried to answer questions properly: he never said, as Aunt Mabel sometimes did, 'Oh run away and don't bother me now.'

He said, 'Sometimes innocent people get arrested, I suppose. But not often – not often in England, anyway.'

Ben said impatiently, 'I don't mean robbers and people like that. I mean important people, like Prime Ministers. Why should a Prime Minister be put in prison?'

Mr Mallory stroked his moustache with his pipe stem. It made a rasping sound. 'I don't think an English Prime Minister has been imprisoned for years – for hundreds of years.'

'I meant an African one.'

Mr Mallory went on stroking his moustache. Then he sighed, took out his pouch and began to fill his pipe, carefully tucking in straggly wisps of tobacco. 'Well, Ben – in some African countries – and in some countries in Europe for that matter – things are much rougher and tougher than they are in England or America. In every country people have different ideas about how they want to be ruled. In England, when politicians disagree, they have a General Election, and the party that gets the most votes, wins. But in some places things aren't so – so tidy. Sometimes the people in power decide to imprison the people who were in power before they were, so they can't oppose them any more. This is very often cruel and stupid, but you must remember that it is the sort of thing that used to happen in England, years ago . . .'

He went on, explaining about Charles I and the Wars of the Roses, but Ben wasn't interested. He wriggled about in his bed and said, 'I don't much like history.'

His father smiled. 'Don't you? Well, you know the things that are happening now will be history one day.'

Ben sighed. This was the sort of thing schoolmasters said. 'What I want to know is – why should an African Prime Minister be in prison in England. *Now*. Not a lot of dull old history.'

'Why do you want to know?' Mr Mallory said. He was smoking his pipe now and his eyes were narrowed because of the smoke. Ben hesitated. He was reluctant to tell his father about Thomas. He would ask too many questions. He would be sure to find out that Thomas was not supposed to have visitors and then he would be sure to say Ben must not go there, in case he got into trouble.

So he said cautiously, 'I read something in the newspapers.' Surely, if what Thomas had told him was true, it would be in the newspapers?

Mr Mallory looked at Ben with a surprised expression. 'I

didn't know you read anything if you could help it. Not that I *mind*, you know ... Still, I know what you're talking about now. You mean this trouble about Chief Okapi ...' He shook his head with a little sigh. 'It's a bad business. A bad business.'

'I *think* that's the right name,' Ben said slowly. He frowned thoughtfully, as his father had done a minute or two ago. He wished he had a pipe and a moustache: it would be useful when he was pretending to think.

'Well, I can explain about *him*,' Mr Mallory said, and Ben settled back comfortably against his pillows. His father's explanations were often very long. Ben hoped he would keep awake.

Until two months ago, Chief Okapi had been the Prime Minister of Tiga. Tiga was a rich country in East Africa, roughly the same size as Kenya, but much richer because there were diamond mines in the high mountains of the north. The land above the mines was ruled by a Chief called Nogola, but the profits from the mines went, by law, to the Tiga government.

For a long time, Tiga had been a peaceful country; the people were prosperous and better fed than in most other countries in Africa. The towns had broad, straight streets lined with jacaranda trees and there were fine hospitals and schools.

The trouble had started with a rumour that Chief Okapi had been keeping some of the money the Government had received from the diamond mine, to make himself richer. Nogola had travelled round the country, stirring up the peaceful people and saying that Chief Okapi was a thief and a traitor. Chief Okapi had sent soldiers to capture him, but Nogola went into hiding in his high, northern mountains with the men who supported him and began to plot to overthrow the Government.

Nogola and his friends were rich; they bought arms in

Egypt and, when they were strong enough, they marched on the capital city. The Government collapsed; Chief Okapi fled to England and Nogola was made Prime Minister instead.

One of the first things he had done was to ask the British Government to send Chief Okapi back to Tiga to stand his trial as a traitor.

'Is he a traitor?' Ben asked eagerly. 'I mean – did he keep the money from the diamonds?'

Mr Mallory puffed at his pipe. 'I shouldn't think so. From all accounts, he's a good man who worked hard for his people. I don't suppose even Nogola believes he's a traitor, but that's not the point . . .'

'What is the point, then?'

'Well – Okapi was liked by the people and Nogola isn't. Since he's been in power he has passed a lot of bad laws and imposed a great many new taxes. The people don't like this – there have been riots in Tiga. Nogola wants Okapi back so he can point to him, so he can say, "Here is this man, Okapi the traitor who has stolen your money and is the cause of all your troubles." He hopes it will make them forget the bad laws and the taxes. Can you understand that, Ben?'

'It's – it's like thinking hard about something else when you've hurt yourself. It takes your mind off the pain. But I don't see why we've put Chief Okapi in prison. He hasn't done anything to us.'

'No.' Mr Mallory hesitated. 'It's a matter of politics. You see, any country can ask another country to send back a fugitive – an escaped criminal. And even if Nogola is a bad man, he is the head of the Government in Tiga now. He has asked for Okapi to be sent back – as a common criminal – to stand his trial. And we have put him in prison until we have decided what to do.'

'But what will happen to him if we do send him back? If they say he's a traitor . . .' Ben felt suddenly icy cold. 'Traitors are shot, aren't they?'

Mr Mallory drew silently on his pipe. Ben got the feeling he did not much want to answer this question. 'I don't know what will happen to him,' he admitted reluctantly. 'No one does.'

Ben sat up in bed and clutched at his father's arm. 'Then we can't send him back.' His voice rose. 'I mean – you can't send someone to – to their *death*.'

'I hope not.' Mr Mallory looked at Ben and smiled. 'Luckily, a lot of people think as you do. They have got up a petition – there are thousands of signatures – and the whole thing is to be settled in Parliament tomorrow.' He squeezed Ben's shoulder and pushed him gently down on to the pillow. 'It's time you went to sleep.'

Ben lay still, feeling he would never sleep again.

'Will his son be sent back too?' he asked in a small voice.

'His son?' Mr Mallory said sharply and for a moment Ben was afraid he had given himself away. Of course it was unlikely that there would have been anything about Thomas in the newspapers. He wasn't important, after all.

But although Mr Mallory looked at Ben in a puzzled way as if there was something here he didn't quite understand, after a moment, he just yawned a little.

'Was there a child?' he said. 'I don't remember.'

After he had gone, Ben lay in the dark listening to the sounds of the night, the creaking of the plane trees outside the open window and the distant hum of the traffic, thinking over what his father had told him. As he lay there, growing sleepier and sleepier in spite of wanting to stay awake, it began to seem more like a story he had read than something that was actually happening. And because in a story nothing very terrible happens to the good people – in the end, anyway – he pushed Chief Okapi to the back of his mind and began to think how exciting it would be to be Thomas: to be a Prime Minister's son and be plotted against, and have to escape. He wondered how they had escaped from Tiga. On foot? On camels? His eyelids drooped and he snuggled his cheek into the pillow. He fell asleep dreaming of silent, shrouded figures, hunched on loping camels, fleeing in the darkness of the night . . .

4

THE ESCAPE FROM TIGA

But it hadn't been like that.

'We got away in the American lady's car,' Thomas said. 'In broad daylight. My father would not go before. Nogola is a bad man and he wanted to stay and fight him but my Uncle Tuku said he must go and take me with him. The Uncles had come in the evening and they had gone on arguing, right through the night. I was there all the time. No one told me to go to bed – there was no one to tell me, my mother had gone to America and the servants had run away and left us quite alone.

'Uncle Joseph said it would be cowardly of my father to go and that anyway we could not, because all the roads out of Tiga were watched. But Uncle Tuku said we must go all the same. He said Uncle Joseph spoke foolishly and that there were times when to run away was the only thing a brave man could do. He said the future of Tiga lay in my father's hands, that soon all the people would see Nogola was a false and wicked man and then my father could come back and govern in peace. He was terribly angry with my Uncle Joseph . . .'

Thomas gave a shiver, although it was warm where they were sitting, in the garden, outside the hut.

'My Uncle Tuku is terrible when he is angry. He is a very strong man. He once killed a lion with his bare hands. He is my father's elder brother and my father always listens to him. In the end, my father said it was no good now; we had waited too long and the morning had come. But Uncle Tuku said he had arranged everything. He left with my Uncle Joseph. They were to drive to the airport along one road and we were to leave by another. My father and I crept out through the garden and an American lady was waiting with her car by the back gate. She is a missionary and a friend of my father and my Uncle Tuku. She is a very small, very fat lady, but she was very kind. She gave me a bar of chocolate and hid me and my father under some coats in the back of the car and drove us straight to the airport where Uncle Tuku had an aeroplane waiting.'

'Didn't anyone stop you?' Ben said, round-eyed.

'Once. The soldiers stopped us. Nogola had got control of the army. We could hear them talking but we lay still under the coats. The American lady laughed and joked with them. They said, wasn't she a friend of Chief Okapi and she laughed very loudly and said that she was not. She said she thought Chief Okapi was a bad man and that she hoped he would be treated as he deserved. I was very afraid then – I thought she would give us up – but my father whispered to me to lie still and quiet. And it was all right. After a little while the soldiers let the car through the barrier they had built across the road and the American lady began to drive very fast. We got out from under the coats and she said, "My God, they're after us."

'I was surprised to hear a missionary say "My God" like that, but then she said, "Dear God, help us," and I saw that she meant it. Because they were coming after us, in a fast car. My father shouted, "Someone must have warned them," and she said, very quietly, "I am afraid there are enemies close to you, Chief Okapi."

'I could see that my father wanted to ask her what she meant but there was no time to talk, she was driving so fast now. Even though my father held on to me tight and he is strong, nearly as strong as my Uncle Tuku, we were thrown about in the back of the car. We drove on to the airfield, right up to the plane, and my father dragged me out of the car and gave me to Uncle Tuku who was waiting there and he carried me into the plane. The plane took off and when we looked down, we could see them waving and shouting. There were about forty soldiers all round the American lady's car, some of our own countrymen and some white mercenaries Nogola had in his army . . .'

'What happened to the American lady?' Ben asked.

'We had to leave her behind. There was room in the plane but she would not come. My father was very worried about her. But Uncle Tuku said she would be all right, because she was a good woman and everyone loved her and because she was an American, too. He said even Nogola would not dare to offend the American Government.' He stopped for a moment and then said, 'It is her brother's house we are living in now. He is a Professor, but he is in America for the moment. We came straight here when we got to England – me, Uncle Joseph, Uncle Tuku, and my father. Then the police came and arrested my father, one night when I was asleep.'

Until he said that, Ben had been feeling rather jealous. Nothing as exciting as this had ever happened to him – or ever would. But when Thomas spoke about his father, it turned a wonderful adventure into something real and frightening.

'It will be dreadful if he is sent home to Tiga,' he said slowly, wondering if Thomas knew what might happen to his father. Perhaps he was too young to understand . . .

'It would be the end of my country. The end of Tiga,' Thomas said quietly. 'There is no one else – no one as good and wise as my father. Not even Uncle Tuku. He is a strong man but he is old – and old-fashioned, my father says. He likes to be agreed with in everything. If he were Prime Minister, he would want to rule completely, like a king or a dictator. He does not understand Parliamentary Government.'

Ben thought this sounded as if Thomas was repeating something someone else had said. He was about to say so when he heard a sound, a long, low whistle that might have been a bird, but was not.

'That's Lil,' Thomas said. He scrambled to his feet and whispered quickly, 'Don't tell her what we have been talking about. It is a secret – a State secret. She might tell someone.'

'Not if she's your friend,' Ben said, shocked.

Thomas grinned. 'She is a woman. All women talk. They cannot help it. Besides, she is too young.'

Ben followed him to the ladder. The girl who stood beside it *was* young, and thin – thin as a heron, Ben thought – with a thin, pale face. Her hair was golden, or would have been if it had been clean, and cut jaggedly round her face. She wore jeans that had rubbed through at the knees and what looked like a man's old sweater, a grey, shapeless garment that draped bulkily on her slender frame.

She showed no surprise at the sight of Ben. She grinned and said, 'Ullo.'

'This is a new friend of mine, Benjamin Mallory,' Thomas said and her grin broadened.

'That's a mouthful and a half, ain't it? I'll call him Ben.'

'Most people do,' Ben said.

'If they didn't, they'd get tired talking to you,' she said pertly, and although he didn't think this very funny, Ben smiled. He thought that behind the grin and the cheeky voice she was probably shy: people who teased you like this as soon as they met you, often were. She was rubbing her hands up and down the sides of her shabby jeans in a nervous way. And it was never pleasant when you came to visit a friend, to find another friend already there . . .

Thomas said, 'I've got you some lunch. Chicken and a bottle of milk. It's in the hut. You'd better come now because I can't stay long. It's Mr Baldry's afternoon.'

'Oh – *him*,' she said. Then she looked at Thomas suspiciously, 'I don't jus' come for the food, you know.'

'I know that,' Thomas said in a gentle voice, rather as if he were talking to a shy, wild animal. She *did* look shy and wild, Ben thought, as if she might dart away like a deer at the first alarming sound.

Thomas went on, 'But you might as well eat it, now it's there.'

'*Mightn't* I?' she said, and her eyes shone. Then she gave a giggle and clapped her hand to her mouth. 'Mustn't wake *her*, must we? The ole dragon. She's sleeping. I took a peek through the railings at the front. She's out to the world, mouth wide open and catching flies.'

'Miss Fisher likes her nap after lunch,' Thomas explained to Ben. He said reprovingly to Lil, 'You should not hang about in the street, though. She might not have been asleep and if she hadn't been, she would have caught you, peeping into the window.'

'Oh, *her*,' said Lil with a swagger. 'Who's scared of her?'

Thomas didn't answer. He just said, 'Come on,' rather crossly and led the way through the bushes to the hut. He went inside and came out with a leg of chicken and a half pint of milk. The bottle was still frosty from the ice-box.

'No plate?' Lil said. 'I like my meals served dainty.' But she swallowed hard and her eyes grew big as she looked at the chicken. Ben thought he had never seen anyone look so hungry, though she tried hard not to show how hungry she was, eating the chicken with small, neat bites and not looking at it in between. She drank the milk from the bottle; when she had finished, she put it down and smiled. There was a milky moustache on her upper lip and her face looked somehow plumper. 'Man, was that *fabulous*,' she said and stretched out contentedly on the dusty grass.

'I tried to get you some ice-cream,' Thomas said. 'But Uncle Joseph came into the kitchen and there wasn't time. I'd already got the chicken stuffed up under my blouse. There's a tin of raspberries for pudding, if you like.'

'Don't like puddings,' she said lazily.

'Haven't you really had any lunch?' Ben could not help asking.

She shook her head. Her eyes had a wary look that warned him not to ask any more questions.

But Thomas said, 'Lil's mother's in hospital. She got knocked down by a car and broke her leg. And her father is a sailor. So she's got no one to look after her.'

'Oh, shut *up*,' Lil said crossly, but she sounded more frightened than angry. Her cheeks had gone very pink.

'It's all right,' Thomas said. 'Ben's a friend. He won't tell anyone.'

'I dunno about that,' she muttered. She sat up, thin hands locked round her knees, and looked at Ben with a steady, unwinking stare. He had the feeling that she was putting him through some kind of test.

'I promise,' he said. 'I mean I don't know what it is you don't want me to tell but I'll promise if you like.'

'Swear,' she said. 'Promising isn't good enough.'

Ben licked his finger and held it up. 'See that wet, see that dry, cut my throat if I tell a lie.' He drew his finger across his throat and produced a highly convincing death rattle.

She gave a little, relaxing sigh. 'All right, then. It's jus' that They think I'm staying wiv my Granny. That's what I told Them, see? Only it wasn't true. I mean I couldn't be wiv my Granny because she's dead.'

This seemed very confusing. 'Who's They?' Ben said.

'The Welfare, o' course,' she said in a surprised voice as if Ben ought to have known. 'When my Mum got knocked down the Welfare lady come and said I couldn't stay in the flat by meself. She said I'd got to go wiv her and she'd take me to a place where they'd look after me till my Mum was better. So I told 'er I was going to me Granny and she went away, but she come back after, snoopin' and pokin' about. She was back this morning, banging on the door and calling through the letter-box.' She screwed up her face and put on a funny, high-pitched voice, ' "Lilian, Lil-i-an de-ar. Be a good little girl and open the door!" Silly mutt. So I jus' bolted it up and nipped out the back.'

Ben said slowly, 'I expect she's worried about you. I mean, if your mother's in hospital, someone ought to look after you.'

'I c'n look after meself.' She glared at Ben and went on in a suddenly indignant voice, 'Well, I couldn't go off wiv her could I? I've got to stay and look after the flat for me Mum. And Joey. That's our budgie. The last thing Mum said to me when they took her off in the ambulance was "look arter Joey for me". She jus' loves that budgie. The Welfare lady said one of the neighbours 'ud look after 'im, but they wouldn't know how. I mean they wouldn't keep his tray nice and clean an' they wouldn't talk to 'im like Mum and I do. He's like – like one of our family. He wouldn't understand if I went off and left 'im – he'd break 'is little heart.'

She looked at Ben, cheeks flaming. He wondered how old she was – not more than eight or nine, he thought.

Thomas said quickly, 'Of course you couldn't.' He looked at Ben. 'It's all right, really it is. You see, her mother will only be away for another fortnight. And she's all right. I mean I can get lots of food so she won't starve. I have been looking after her.'

Lil gave a sudden, scornful snort. '*You've* bin looking after *me*. I like that! That's rich!' She started to laugh and then stopped.

All three froze into stillness as they heard Miss Fisher call. 'Thomas, Thomas . . .'

He jumped to his feet. 'I expect Mr Baldry has come. If you like, you can both stay here. Though I may not be able to come back . . .'

'Thomas. *Thomas.*'

He grinned at them and ran off, towards the house.

Lil sat still, thoughtfully chewing grass. Now Thomas was gone, Ben felt slightly shy of her. Although she was so much younger than he was, she looked very tough and competent and sure of herself.

Suddenly she said, 'D'you want to watch ole Thomas? It's ever so comical. Like something on telly.'

'Won't they see us?'

She shook her head, grinning. 'You come along of me.'

She got to her feet, stretched, and walked back to the ladder. She was very quick and light; she was up and over the wall like a cat. Once on the other side, she led Ben along by the side of the wall to where there was a tumble-down shed. They climbed on to the roof of the shed and from there they could reach the lower branches of a tall plane tree. Lil climbed quickly up into it – so quickly, that even Ben, who was neat and sure-footed, had difficulty in following her. In fact, at one point, she disappeared from view. He hesitated, standing in a fork of the tree, and then heard her low giggle from somewhere above him. Then her face appeared among the leaves – one wide grin, like the Cheshire cat in *Alice*. 'Put your foot on that branch, stupid.' He did as she told him, swung himself higher, and found she was standing on a sort of platform, in the tree. Carefully she parted some leafy twigs. 'Look ...' she said softly.

The tree hung over the wall, right into Thomas's garden, and they could see Thomas quite clearly. He was doing exercises on a mat on the patchy lawn while a short, bald man in white trousers and singlet counted, 'One, two, three, *one*, two and thrreee.'

Miss Fisher sat in a wicker chair on the fire-escape outside the french windows. She was reading the newspaper.

Someone was playing a gramophone somewhere.

The bald man was very bald. The skin on the top of his

head was pale pink and shiny. He was short and thick set and strong: while they watched, he did a beautiful somersault in the air and landed, bouncing, on the balls of his feet. Then he caught Thomas round the waist and whirled him round. They could hear Thomas laugh.

The exercises began again. One, two, three, *one*, two and thrreee. Miss Fisher snoozed over her newspaper, the gramophone played. Somewhere inside the house, a telephone began to ring. Then it stopped and the gramophone stopped too. Miss Fisher looked up from her newspaper and Thomas and Mr Baldry stopped the exercises. They all turned towards the french windows. They were all very still as if they were waiting for something important to happen.

'What is it?' Ben whispered.

Lil shrugged her skinny shoulders. 'Search me.'

They seemed to wait for a long time, though it could not have been more than a few minutes before two men came out through the french windows on to the fire-escape. They were both dark-skinned, both Africans, but there the resemblance ended. One man was small and wearing an ordinary suit. The other was tall and big and dressed in tribal costume: one enormous, silky, brown shoulder was bare, the rest of his body was covered by a magnificent red blanket, patterned in blue and gold.

'They must be the Uncles,' Ben said. 'The one in the blanket must be Uncle Tuku. He *looks* as if he could kill a lion with his bare hands.'

The big man looked up, almost as if he had heard, though Ben had spoken very softly. Then he beckoned to Thomas who ran up the iron steps of the fire-escape and they disappeared into the house together. The other African – Uncle Joseph, Ben thought – spoke to Miss Fisher who got up from her chair. She followed Thomas and Uncle Tuku indoors and Uncle Joseph came slowly down the steps and strolled across the lawn to where Mr Baldry was standing. They walked up and down together, talking earnestly. From the tree Ben could see very little of them except the top of their heads: one so black and woolly, the other so glistening and bald.

Thomas did not appear again. Ben began to be bored. He was just about to suggest that they climbed down the tree, when Lil said something instead. Something rather odd.

'It's true what I said. I don't jus' come for the food. I come to keep an eye on 'im. I don't trust 'im.'

'Who?' Ben said, astonished. 'Thomas?'

''Course not, stupid.' She tossed her head scornfully and pointed down, through the leaves. '*Him*. Old Baldy . . .'

5

'ARE YOU AFRAID, THOMAS?'

About your friend,' Mr Mallory began, and then stopped. The fat had spat up from the pan in which he was frying bacon and sausages for Ben's supper and stung his cheek. He rubbed at his skin with his handkerchief and sighed.

Some men are good cooks. Mr Mallory was not. However hard he concentrated, the food he produced was either raw or burned to a cinder. Looking at him as he prodded unhappily at a sausage that had turned coal black on one side and remained obstinately pink on the other, Ben thought that it was probably a good thing, on the whole, that he was marrying Miss Mackingtosh.

Mr Mallory tipped the burnt bacon and the half-cooked sausage on to a cold plate. He heaved another sigh and wiped his forehead with his handkerchief as if he had just completed a long and difficult task. 'I'm afraid it doesn't look very appetising,' he said.

Though Ben could eat most things, he looked at his plate with misgivings. 'I expect I can fill up on cornflakes,' he said helpfully.

'You'd better have some milk,' his father said. 'Thank goodness you don't have to cook milk. I wish I could take you out to dinner with me tonight but it's not possible. I'd arranged to meet this client before I knew you'd be staying on.'

'I don't mind being alone,' Ben said.

'Sure? Not scared or anything?'

' 'Course not. I never am.' This sounded boastful, so he added, 'I'm not being brave or anything. Being alone just isn't one of the things I'm frightened about.'

'Good.' Mr Mallory stood by the table watching Ben eat, but as he was thinking about something else he didn't notice when Ben hid a particularly charred sausage under a piece of bread. Ben glanced up slyly, but his father's eyes held an absent expression and he was stroking his moustache with his pipe stem.

At last he said, 'Ah yes – I remember what I meant to tell you. About your friend, Chief Okapi. It looks as if things are going to turn out all right. Nothing definite, exactly, but the odds are that he'll be released quite soon.'

'*Oh*,' Ben said. He felt his cheeks grow hot with excitement and pleasure.

'It was a very interesting debate in the House. You see, Ben . . .'

Mr Mallory launched into a long explanation about something called Precedent and the special problem of Emergent Nations, but it sounded uncomfortably like a lesson and Ben barely listened.

'So he won't be sent back to be tried as a traitor?' he broke in, cutting his father off in mid-sentence.

'Well . . . no,' Mr Mallory said. Though he smiled, he sounded rather disappointed that Ben was not more interested in the other things he had been saying. He lit his pipe and said, 'As a matter of fact, the whole thing is rather secret. It's not been generally announced yet. It was just luck that I happened to find out from a man I know. So keep it under your hat. Don't go shouting it from the rooftops or ringing up the newspapers.'

'I wouldn't do that,' Ben said seriously.

Mr Mallory laughed and rumpled his hair.

'Somehow I didn't think you would. Well – be a good boy, go to bed early.' He looked at his watch and picked up his brief-case. 'Duty calls,' he said.

'Why is it secret?' Ben said suddenly as his father opened the flat door.

'There are reasons.' Mr Mallory hesitated. 'Too complicated. You wouldn't understand.'

'Oh, but I would,' Ben began eagerly, wishing he had been more attentive earlier because then his father would have been more willing to stop and explain.

But Mr Mallory just smiled and closed the door.

It was dark when Ben reached Thomas's garden. A little wind was rustling the trees, high up in the top branches, but down on the ground everything was still and very quiet. A twig, cracking under Ben's foot, sounded sharp and loud as a pistol shot.

He stood in the bushes feeling uncertain. He had not really thought what he was going to do. He only knew that he wanted to find Thomas and tell him his father was safe. Even if it was a secret, Thomas should know it. To tell him was not the same as telling the newspapers – though of course Dad had only meant that as a joke. He would not think it mattered if Thomas knew. Thomas was only a boy and not important . . .

Ben moved cautiously towards the house. All the windows were dark; black squares in the blackness of the house wall.

Ben stood at the foot of the fire-escape, looking up. Perhaps he could find Thomas's bedroom. Thomas was almost certain to be in bed by now. Miss Fisher wasn't the sort of woman to let a boy stay up late. If he could find Thomas's bedroom he could tell him the good news and go straight home, quick and silent as a thief in the night ...

But as he climbed the first flight of rusty, iron stairs, Ben's heart was pounding. It was not so easy. Suppose Miss Fisher were to catch him – or one of the Uncles. The terrible Uncle Tuku in his Chief's robes! Ben thought about Uncle Tuku and moved more slowly; with each step he took his feet seemed to grow heavier until it was like heaving up two balls of lead. Once he kicked a little stone that had somehow got on to the fire-escape and it rattled down and down with a dreadful, ear-splitting, heart-stopping sound. Ben stood still, half expecting all the windows in the house to blaze suddenly with light. None of them did. But in one of the other houses in the row, someone flung up a sash window and a radio blared out a man's voice, singing a sad, sobbing tune. Ben listened to the song and, in a strange way, felt more confident. Perhaps it was just that the singing made him feel less alone.

On the first floor, the lower half of a window was open. He peered in. It was dark inside and the drawn curtains were heavy and thick, moving only very little in the light breeze. For a moment he waited, shivering, although the night was warm. Then he thought of Thomas, lying awake in the dark and worrying about his father, and pulled himself up, over the window-sill.

As his feet touched the floor inside the room, the light was switched on.

He stood, so rigid with fright that for a moment or two, though he heard voices, he had no idea what they were saying. He just closed his eyes and waited – waited for the curtains to be torn open, for the certain discovery.

But nothing happened. Cautiously, he opened his eyes. He

was standing in a small window recess, closed in by the curtains. Just in front of him was a gap where they did not meet properly.

Through this gap, he could see Thomas. He was sitting in a red, velvet chair, his head resting against the back. His eyes looked sleepy and unfocused. He was wearing rumpled pyjamas as if he had just got out of bed.

Uncle Tuku was sitting opposite him on a straight, hard chair. His back was half turned towards the window so that Ben could only see his massive shoulders covered with the rich blanket, his rough, scarred cheek and grizzled, crinkly mop of hair.

The other Uncle – Uncle Joseph who had walked with Old Baldy in the garden – looked much more ordinary. He had a cheerful, round face, a broad nose and a great many shining, white teeth that showed even though he wasn't smiling. He was perched on a table, swinging his legs and looking at Uncle Tuku.

Ben stayed where he was. There was nothing else he could do.

Uncle Tuku had a low, rumbling, thundery voice. 'Explain to me,' he was saying. 'Explain to me, Joseph.'

Uncle Joseph shrugged his shoulder so slightly that the movement was barely perceptible. His expression – Ben recognized it at once – was what schoolmasters call 'insolent'.

'I have explained, Tuku. The detective was asleep in the kitchen. I found him there. He should have been watching the house. Anything might have happened.' His voice rose. He sounded indignant – *no*, Ben thought suddenly, he was *trying* to sound indignant . . .

Uncle Tuku said, 'I cannot understand it. Was it wise to dismiss him, Joseph? It is not easy to get men we can trust.' He sounded more worried than angry.

Uncle Joseph said, 'We cannot trust a man to watch the house if he falls asleep in the kitchen. Too much is at stake.

We have someone to take his place. I have spoken to Mr Baldry. He is strong and reliable. Thomas will be safe with him.'

Thomas sat up. His eyes were not sleepy now. He said nothing but he looked at Uncle Tuku.

Uncle Tuku said slowly, 'We know so little about Mr Baldry. Is it safe to leave the boy in his care?'

'You have to trust people sometimes,' Uncle Joseph said gently. 'Even you cannot be everywhere, Tuku. And if you do not trust Mr Baldry, do you also not trust me? The boy is my concern, as he is yours.'

Uncle Tuku bowed his heavy head. 'I am sorry, Joseph. I did not mean to insult you.'

'I am not easily insulted,' Uncle Joseph said lightly. 'I understand. The important thing is Thomas and his safety.'

'Exactly,' Uncle Tuku said. 'Thomas – come here.'

Thomas got out of the red velvet chair – reluctantly, Ben thought – and walked towards his uncle who took his small hands in his large ones and held him between his knees.

He said, 'You must listen to me, Thomas. We have already talked a great deal and soon you can go back to your bed and rest. But before you do that, I must know that you understand the part you have to play. That you understand – with your heart, as well as your mind – the heavy matters we have been discussing.'

Thomas did not move or speak. His eyes were fixed on his uncle's face.

Uncle Joseph swung himself off the table. He was looking at Thomas with pity.

'Don't alarm the child too much,' he said and walked towards the window. 'It's stuffy in here,' he said and stretched out his hand towards the curtain.

Ben caught his breath.

Uncle Tuku said in a loud, commanding voice, 'Joseph,' and Uncle Joseph stopped. Uncle Tuku had turned towards the windows so that Ben could see him more clearly now. He had a broad, strong face – alarming in its strength and in the wicked-looking blue scars that ran down either cheek. He was old: his bristling white eyebrows looked strange against his dark skin.

'Thomas is no longer a child,' he said, very sternly. 'He is almost a man. It is time he learned to behave like a man.'

Uncle Joseph did not reply. He looked, Ben thought, as if he would like to say something but did not dare.

Uncle Tuku said, 'Thomas, listen to me.' He spoke slowly, pausing between each sentence. 'Praise the Lord, your father is to be released. In a few days – maybe within the week – he will be allowed to proceed to America. He will be in no danger during that time because the British Government will be watching over him and Nogola does not want trouble with the British. Do you understand that?'

Thomas nodded. He had a stiff, hypnotized look.

Uncle Tuku went on. 'Nogola has many friends. Not only in Tiga, but here, in England. Wicked men who have no love for Tiga, but only for the riches of her diamond mines. The desire for wealth is an evil thing and it corrupts men's souls. And every man who befriends Nogola, for their own gain, is your father's enemy. They hate your father because he has used the money from the mine for the good of the people of Tiga. They are afraid of him too, because they know that when he returns to power he will punish them and take their riches away. Frightened men are desperate men, Thomas. If they cannot strike at your father directly, they will strike at him through you. If they could kidnap you and take you back to Tiga, they know your father would return. His love for you is great – greater than it should be. If he believed you were in danger, he would forget everything – our country, our future . . .'

Thomas gave a little gasp and tried to pull away but Uncle Tuku held him firmly. 'You *must* listen, Thomas. I will not always be here.' He paused and added gravely, 'You must go nowhere alone. You must trust no one. No one.'

There was a long silence. Then he said, 'Are you afraid, Thomas?'

After a minute, Thomas answered in a high, light voice, 'I am not afraid, Uncle Tuku.'

Uncle Tuku lifted his head. His voice was a roar – like an old lion's. 'Then you should be. You should be very afraid. Not for yourself, because you are not important. Only our country is important, and your father. No man should ever be afraid for himself. But he should always be afraid for his country.'

Thomas's eyes were glistening. He was trying hard not to cry.

Uncle Tuku said, slowly and heavily, 'You must swear to me, Thomas. You must swear that you will never forget to be afraid.'

Ben saw that there were little beads of perspiration on his face. The room was very quiet. Thomas stood still. Uncle Joseph stood still, his head thrust forward, watching. Ben was so absorbed in the scene that he had quite forgotten that he had no right to be here. His eyes were fixed on Thomas who suddenly seemed to draw himself up, very straight and tall.

He said, 'I swear, Uncle Tuku.' And then the tears began to pour down his face.

Uncle Joseph muttered something under his breath. Uncle Tuku released Thomas and Joseph put an arm round his shaking shoulders and led him back to the red velvet chair. Uncle Tuku stood up – standing, he was massive, a colossus – and looked down at Thomas with a thoughtful expression on his face. Ben thought, a little indignantly, that he did not look at all sorry.

Uncle Joseph said, 'Have you finished, Tuku?' and Uncle Tuku nodded. 'I will fetch Miss Fisher, then,' Uncle Joseph said, and left the room.

The room was silent now, except for the little sobs that Thomas could not control. Uncle Tuku stood like a statue, staring straight in front of him. When Miss Fisher came in, he turned his head slowly and looked at her.

Miss Fisher looked at Thomas and clicked her tongue against her teeth. She went over to him and helped him out of the chair. 'Come along, you must get to your bed now.' She put her hand on his shoulder, not ungently, and pushed him out through the door.

Uncle Tuku said, 'Miss Fisher,' and she turned.

She said, in a calm voice, 'This is really too bad. I shall have no end of trouble getting him to sleep . . .'

Ben was astonished that she should dare to speak to Uncle Tuku like this.

Uncle Tuku sounded weary. 'Miss Fisher – the boy has to be made to understand. *You* must understand too. He must be watched night and day.'

She said, 'That's as may be. But I don't see the point in upsetting the child. The poor little chap. Oh – I know it's a lot of old politics, but what has a child got to do with politics?'

Uncle Tuku said quietly, 'Miss Fisher, in my country we have a proverb. "When two elephants fight, it is the grass that suffers."'

She frowned: Ben wondered if she understood what he meant. He didn't. Then she said, 'Grass doesn't have feelings, Mr Tuku. Children do.'

And she tossed her head and marched out of the door.

Ben thought Uncle Tuku would never go. He stood motionless in the middle of the room and Ben stood motionless behind the curtain. He began to be dreadfully afraid that he might sneeze and give himself away, and once he had started to think about it, the tickle started in the back of his nose. He clasped his fingers over his mouth to stop it, screwing up his face until his eyes streamed water. Then, just as he was beginning to think he could hold back the sneeze no longer, Uncle Tuku sighed – a deep, gusty sigh like the wind in a tunnel – and went out of the room. Ben gasped, tumbled over the window-sill and clattered down the fire-escape. He was so relieved that he did not care how much noise he made. He ran through the garden and swarmed up the ladder. He didn't know how he got over the wall without cutting himself to ribbons, but he did. Nor, really, how he got home, his legs were shaking so . . .

Mr Mallory was not yet home. Ben crawled into bed and pulled the clothes right over his head. For the first time in his life, his bed seemed just about the pleasantest place in the world.

6

THE STRANGE BEHAVIOUR OF
UNCLE JOSEPH

From the front, Thomas's house looked like all the other houses in the street, tall, narrow and shabby. The only difference was that it was not divided into flats; there was no row of bells on the front door, only a gleaming brass knocker. The knocker swung as Uncle Joseph opened the door and stood at the top of the steps, looking up the road as if he were waiting for someone.

Ben, who was on the opposite pavement, slipped into the doorway of a sweet shop and pretended to be interested in the display of ice-cream cartons in the dusty, neglected window. Though he was doing nothing wrong, and Uncle Joseph was not an alarming person like Uncle Tuku, Ben did not want to be seen by him.

When he thought about the night before, it set his heart

thumping. In an odd way he was much more afraid, thinking about it, than he had been at the time. *Then* he had been too taken up with what was happening to be really frightened except, perhaps, at the beginning when he had stepped into the room and at the end, when he was running home. But ever since he had woken up this morning he had been re-enacting the scene in his mind and torturing himself with wondering what would have happened if Uncle Joseph had opened the curtains and found him, or if, later on, he had sneezed and Uncle Tuku ... It didn't bear thinking about but he couldn't help it. It was rather like having a sore tooth and having to prod it occasionally to make sure it was there.

Besides being frightened, he was also a little ashamed. Last night, hiding behind the curtain, he had been a sort of spy. He ought not to have spied on them last night. He ought not to be spying now ...

All the same, he stood in the sweet shop doorway and watched the house side-long. It was rather stupid, really. What was he expecting would happen? Real life wasn't like a story, with something new and exciting on every page.

Certainly, nothing seemed to be happening at the moment. There was only Uncle Joseph, yawning and stretching himself outside the front door as if he were enjoying the sun. And Mr Baldry coming along on his bicycle ...

Mr Baldry. Old Baldy. The sun glinted on the pink dome of his head as he swung off his bicycle and left it standing against the kerb. He was wearing a long tweed jacket and grey flannels that hung baggily over his cycle clips. He ran lightly up the steps, spoke to Uncle Joseph, and ran down again. As he got back on his bicycle, his shiny, pale face was smiling.

Uncle Joseph went into the house. The knocker swung as he banged the front door behind him.

Nothing happened. The street slept in the sun.

A postman walked from house to house delivering letters.

It was so quiet that Ben could hear the creak of his shoes. A sash window rattled up in the house next door to Thomas's and a woman leant out, shaking a yellow duster. Someone started to practise piano scales.

Ben shifted restlessly from one foot to the other.

Thomas's front door opened again. This time, it was Miss Fisher in a black coat buttoned up to the neck and a black hat set squarely on her square, white forehead. She was carrying a shopping basket and set off down the street.

Well, there was nothing remarkable about *that*.

Then Uncle Joseph came out. He stood on the steps and looked in Miss Fisher's direction. He closed the front door and set off after her.

There was nothing remarkable about that either, until a little way down the road, Miss Fisher crossed over and went into a greengrocer's shop. And then Uncle Joseph stopped. He glanced behind him and stepped into the doorway of a tobacconist. He didn't go inside, he was just waiting there, waiting and watching as Ben had been doing. Then, when Miss Fisher came out of the greengrocer's and continued down the road, Uncle Joseph followed her.

Moving softly on his plimsolled feet, Ben followed *him*.

Miss Fisher was a fast, steady walker. She was also a woman who clearly had set ideas about where she should do her shopping. She preferred little shops to big shops and shops in shabby side-streets to shops in the big, main thoroughfare. Perhaps she had always been used to saving a penny here and a penny there and the habit remained, even when she was spending someone else's money. Whenever she went into a shop, Uncle Joseph stopped and waited and, a little way behind him, Ben stopped and waited too. He admired the way Uncle Joseph always found something to do while he was waiting – not just looking in shop windows, but tying a shoe-lace, lighting a cigarette, or studying a bus timetable on a lamp standard. No one, Ben thought, would ever suspect him of following anyone. He looked like a man out for a gentle stroll in the fine, hot sunshine.

They walked on, through a maze of little streets, and nothing happened except that Miss Fisher's shopping bag grew bulkier and bulkier. Then the street they were in took a sudden turn and opened out into the ring road round the Park. Miss Fisher walked smartly across the pedestrian crossing. Uncle Joseph followed her, but by the time Ben reached the kerb, the traffic had begun to move. Ben fretted on the pavement.

By the time he was able to cross, Uncle Joseph had vanished. But he could still see Miss Fisher, straight-backed and determined, walking into the Park over the tree-shaded canal. She seemed sure, as she had been sure when she was shopping, exactly where she wanted to go. Though the paths were winding and pleasant, she marched along with military briskness, like a soldier on parade. When she reached a small, gravelled square with a sundial in the middle and seats placed at intervals among the rhododendron bushes, she set her basket on the ground and sat down. She leaned back on the seat, unbuttoned her coat, closed her eyes and settled down to a comfortable snooze.

Ben approached her slowly, but she did not move or look up.

He saw that she was really quite old. Her brown hair must be dyed because there were a great many stiff, very white hairs bristling out of her chin. The flesh under her chin was pouchy and soft and her hands, lying limply in her lap, had brown spots on them like a very old lady's hands.

Ben sighed. There was no point in staying here, watching Miss Fisher sleep . . .

He had walked out of the square, on to one of the winding paths, when he heard the crunch of feet on gravel. He slipped into the green, damp cave under a rhododendron bush and peeped through the branches. Uncle Joseph was in the square, bending over Miss Fisher and smiling. He said, 'What a surprise, Miss Fisher! I did not expect to find *you* here.'

His astonishment sounded so genuine that for a startled moment Ben thought he must have been dreaming and that Uncle Joseph hadn't followed Miss Fisher to the Park but had just strolled there, on his own, and come upon her by chance.

Uncle Joseph hitched up his trouser legs and sat beside Miss Fisher. He said, 'The Park is very beautiful at this time of year. I have always found the late summer, in England, one of the most charming seasons. So mellow and golden. Don't you agree?'

'It's very nice,' Miss Fisher said. She sounded rather flustered, which was understandable. She had found a quiet place for her little nap and had not expected to be woken up by one of her employers in order to talk about the weather.

'And the flowers,' Uncle Joseph said. 'Look at all those late roses.' He smiled gently. 'Nature is very wonderful. Do you often come here to enjoy its beauties, Miss Fisher?'

'I sometimes come here for a bit of peace on my time off,' Miss Fisher said. Then, as if she was afraid this had sounded as if she was annoyed with Uncle Joseph for disturbing her, she added, 'At my age, you find children tiring. Not that Thomas is naughty, but he *is* a responsibility. Sometimes I can't sleep at nights for worrying about what Mr Tuku would say if anything should happen to him.'

'I hope it hasn't worried you too much,' Uncle Joseph said. 'There is really no need. To tell you the truth, I think Tuku is making a mountain out of a molehill. I don't really believe there is any danger to the boy.'

'Are you sure?' Miss Fisher said. Her expression, as she turned her head to look at Uncle Joseph, was rather puzzled, Ben thought.

'Quite sure, Miss Fisher. The truth is, that Tuku is old and – and *fussy*.' Uncle Joseph gave a little giggle. 'How he would roar if he heard me say that! But it is true. And there is another thing. He has lived through so many dangers, so many up-heavals and revolutions, that he cannot realize we are living in more peaceful times. He is still living in a world of plots and counter-plots – rather like someone in a boy's adventure story.'

'I thought you had just had a revolution in your country,' Miss Fisher said, rather sharply.

Uncle Joseph spread out his hands. 'There has been a change of Government, Miss Fisher. Do you call it a revolution if you have a change of Government in England?'

Miss Fisher sighed. 'I don't know anything about politics.'

Uncle Joseph laughed. 'Why should you? Women should not trouble their pretty heads with such things. But I can tell you one thing. The only danger to Thomas comes from Tuku himself.' He spoke slowly and impressively. 'Not that Tuku would willingly harm the boy . . .'

'He's not very fond of him, though, is he?' Miss Fisher said.

'No. Tuku is not really *fond* of anyone.' Uncle Joseph shook his head sadly. 'But that is not the point. The point is that Tuku is so concerned – so obsessed with the idea that he is surrounded by enemies, that I am afraid it may have a bad effect upon Thomas. He is a very sensitive boy. I am afraid if he has to spend much more time in London, with his uncle, the effect may be – well – disastrous. I do not think it would be exaggerating to say that the boy might become really ill.'

'I don't think so,' Miss Fisher said flatly. 'Thomas is a very sensible boy.'

There was a silence.

Uncle Joseph sighed. 'I hope you're right,' he said.

Miss Fisher's voice was a little worried. 'Even if I'm not, there's nothing we can do about it, is there?'

Uncle Joseph looked at her. Then he said, 'There *is* some-thing . . . I would like to take Thomas out of London. Into the country. Where he could run about as a boy should do and enjoy the beauties of Nature. It would do him so much good. But Tuku won't hear of it.'

'So that's that, isn't it?' Miss Fisher said.

But she sounded as if she felt uneasy, Ben thought. He felt uneasy too, though he couldn't have explained why.

Uncle Joseph said, 'Not altogether. Of course I could not hope to – er – rescue Thomas without Tuku's permission. And Tuku is always with him during your time off.' He stopped. 'But with your help, Miss Fisher . . .'

Miss Fisher stood up. Ben could not see her face but her back was stiff with outrage. 'Certainly not,' she said. 'Mr Tuku employed me and gave me specific instructions. It would be . . .'

'For the boy's own good,' put in Uncle Joseph quickly.

'That's just your opinion, isn't it?'

'Yes.' Uncle Joseph laughed, merrily. 'But I think I am right. I wish I could convince you . . .'

'You can't,' she said, and picked up her shopping bag.

'Allow *me*.' Uncle Joseph took it from her. 'I'll carry it back.'

'Thank you. It *is* rather heavy.' She hesitated. 'When I took the job, I did not know I would be expected to do the shopping too.'

'I am afraid you are finding it rather tiring,' Uncle Joseph said.

'I'm not a young woman.'

Uncle Joseph smiled, showing most of his teeth. 'I suppose you will be thinking of retiring soon.'

'I can't afford to retire. I – I have an invalid sister. She had a motor accident five years ago and damaged her back. She has a little money, but not enough. And there is no one else to help her but me.'

Uncle Joseph shook his head sadly. 'That is a great shame. I must say, I admire you, Miss Fisher. I would like to think that someone like you – so good and kind and hard-working – could look forward to peace and comfort in the evening of her days. A little cottage, perhaps, where your sister could be with you. A little cottage with a thatched roof and roses round the door . . .'

He spoke enthusiastically. He was a very imaginative man, Ben thought.

'Of course, that *would* be nice,' Miss Fisher said. The look she gave Uncle Joseph was startled and questioning.

'Ah, dreams, dreams . . .' he said in a throbbing, actor's voice. Then he took Miss Fisher's arm and they walked away.

They walked slowly, talking earnestly. Ben followed them, rather half-heartedly because he thought they were going straight home and that he would never get close enough again to hear their conversation.

But they didn't go straight home. They stopped in a side-street and went into a small café. Ben looked through the window and watched them, sitting down at a table.

There was no one else in the café except a thin waitress in a dirty apron who came over to their table with her ordering pad, clicking her pencil against her teeth.

Miss Fisher was looking happy and excited as if she was enjoying this little treat. She studied the menu carefully and Uncle Joseph watched her, smiling.

Ben fidgeted. He wanted terribly to hear what they were going to talk about but he did not want them to see him. Then he saw that it didn't really matter if they *did*. After all, they didn't know him – if he walked into the café they would probably not look at him twice! Grown-ups seldom noticed children unless they were rude or got in their way.

So he walked in, boldly, and sat at a table. The thin waitress brought him a menu and he ordered a strawberry ice.

When the ice came, he ate it slowly, staring out of the window as if he were not at all interested in Uncle Joseph and Miss Fisher, sitting about five feet away from him.

To his disappointment, they were talking so softly that he

could only catch a word or two. Once Miss Fisher said something that sounded like, 'I couldn't face him,' and at once Uncle Joseph broke in with a long, muttered speech that sounded vaguely reassuring. Who couldn't she face, Ben wondered? Then she said one other thing that he was able to hear. After Uncle Joseph had finished speaking she said, quite clearly, 'As long as no harm comes to him,' and this time, Ben was sure that 'him' meant Thomas.

At this point, to Ben's horror, Uncle Joseph turned and looked at him. Ben lowered his head and pretended to be completely absorbed in scraping the liquid dregs of ice-cream out of the glass dish. Uncle Joseph said something quietly to Miss Fisher and she answered him. Ben caught the end of the sentence. '. . . only a child,' she said.

She got up from her chair and spoke to the waitress who was sitting on a stool behind the counter, twiddling the ends of her hair and gazing into the distance. She said, 'It's out the back, dear.'

Miss Fisher disappeared, presumably to the Ladies, and Uncle Joseph sat on, gazing thoughtfully out of the window.

Ben waited. He was not anxious to call attention to himself by getting up and leaving the café. He took his little horse, Pin, out of his pocket and stroked him gently, the way he often did when he was trying to think.

What was Uncle Joseph *at*? Did he really want to 'rescue' Thomas from Uncle Tuku? Although Ben thought Uncle Joseph a much pleasanter person than Uncle Tuku – much jollier and much, much more fond of Thomas – there was something very strange in his behaviour. Perhaps what he said was true. Perhaps he did think it would be best for Thomas to get away from Uncle Tuku and live in the country. And yet – and yet, if Thomas was in the country, wouldn't it be easier for his father's enemies to get hold of him? There were fewer policemen in the country and not so many people about . . .

On the other hand, Uncle Joseph had said Thomas wasn't

in any danger, that he didn't believe his father *had* any enemies here. Ben thought he could not quite believe this. Even though Uncle Tuku had frightened Thomas last night, it hadn't seemed as if he were frightening him for fun. Uncle Tuku wasn't that sort of man. Nor was he the sort of man who told lies. And if what Uncle Joseph had said was true, he would have to be one or the other . . .

Suddenly, Ben's eye was caught. A man had got off a bicycle on the other side of the street and stood looking towards the café. Then he walked purposefully across the road and stood outside the window, opposite the table where Uncle Joseph was sitting.

It was Old Baldy. For a moment, he appeared to be examining the menu that was pasted on the window. Then, very slowly, he lifted his head and looked at Uncle Joseph. It was the first time Ben had seen Old Baldy close to and there was something about his face that sent a chill down his spine. It was a cold, sinister face, very smooth and pinky-brown with two cold, hard eyes like chips of pale marble. He looked at Uncle Joseph and Uncle Joseph looked at him. Then Uncle Joseph jerked up his hand and gave a 'thumbs-up' sign.

7

'IT IS TOO LATE'

Ben was running. His breath came in hard, painful gasps and there was a stitch like a sharp knife in his side. He had been running ever since he left the café. He wanted to get to Thomas before Uncle Joseph and Miss Fisher. He had made up his mind. He was going to march straight up to the front door, bold as brass, and ask to speak to Thomas. Even if Uncle Tuku was there, he couldn't *do* anything to him. He might not even be angry. Surely, there was no harm in Thomas just being friends with another boy?

Perhaps, though, it might be better to pretend that he didn't know Thomas. He could say that he had lost his ball in their garden – this had the advantage of being partly true – and perhaps, if he asked politely, he would be allowed through the house to look for it. Uncle Tuku might be fussy, but he couldn't be as fussy as that. He would see Ben wasn't an enemy. He might even let Thomas go into the garden too, to help look for the ball.

Suddenly, it all seemed absurdly easy. Ben felt almost light-hearted as he reached the end of his street and sprinted along the pavement. But just before he got to Thomas's house, a taxi drew up and Miss Fisher stepped out of it. Ben almost collided with her. He *did* collide with her shopping basket which she had set down on the pavement while she took her purse out of her black handbag: he tripped over the basket and sprawled headlong.

He scrambled to his feet at once, scarlet in the face. 'I'm s-sorry,' he stammered.

'I hope you didn't hurt yourself,' she said, quite kindly, though to Ben's relief she barely glanced at him as he scooped up a cauliflower and a packet of biscuits from the pavement and stuffed them back into the basket. She was busy paying off the taxi-driver: by the time she had snapped her handbag shut, Ben had run on.

But she looked after him. Her eyes watched him until he bolted up the steps of his own house and in through the front door. And there was a puzzled expression on her face as if she was trying to remember where she had seen him before.

Mr Mallory had left cold ham and tomatoes for Ben's lunch. He ate slowly, not tasting anything. It was a bit of luck Miss Fisher hadn't recognized him – he was sure she hadn't – but now she was back, he dared not go to the front door. Perhaps Thomas would be in the garden this afternoon. But even if he was there, someone might be with him. What was it Uncle Tuku had said? *The boy must be watched night and day.*

Ben drank a pint of milk and sat on the kitchen table, swinging his legs and frowning. Somehow – somehow, he must get to Thomas and warn him.

But warn him of what?

It didn't, when you thought about it, amount to very much. Just that queer conversation in the park and then the sign Uncle Joseph had made to Old Baldy. *That* was the really sinister thing – Ben had been convinced when he saw it that those two were plotting something and that Uncle Joseph had wanted to tell Old Baldy that Miss Fisher was on their side – but would it sound so strange and sinister if he reported it to Thomas? What could he say? *Your uncle saw Old Baldy through the window and held up his thumb?* It might be the way they always greeted each other.

And if there *was* a plot, what was it? Just a plan to get Thomas away from Uncle Tuku and into the country? Uncle Joseph might be a kind man and fond of his nephew but he couldn't be *that* kind or *that* fond. After all, it wasn't as if Thomas was being beaten or starved in Uncle Tuku's care . . .

If there was a plot, then, it must be something more serious. Yet how could it be? Because if Uncle Joseph was a kind man, he couldn't mean Thomas any real harm, could he?

No, perhaps not. And yet, Uncle Joseph had followed Miss Fisher to the park and . . . Ben sighed. He seemed to be going round in circles. The more he thought about it, the sillier it seemed. Perhaps, as Uncle Joseph had said about Uncle Tuku, he was just making a mountain out of a molehill. Should he tell Thomas? Should he tell Thomas about it?

Though he thought for nearly an hour, while he ate a bowl of apples and a whole tin of biscuits, Ben could not make up his mind.

*

For the moment, it was made up for him. He couldn't tell Thomas anything, because Thomas wasn't there. Ben waited by the hut for a while, then he crawled through the bushes until he got a good view of the house, but the only person he saw was Old Baldy.

He was sitting on the steps of the fire-escape in his white singlet and shorts, knitting. He was using several balls of different coloured wools. His needles went click-click in a business-like way and he counted aloud. 'Three red, two pink, one fawn, three green . . .' His stubby fingers were quick and neat as he manipulated the coloured wools.

Behind him the french windows were open and someone was practising the piano, inexpertly. Ben wondered if Thomas was having a piano lesson.

Ben wriggled on his stomach back to the wall. He had climbed over it when he heard Lil's whistle. She was up in her tree, sitting astride a low branch. Ben climbed up to her.

'Have you seen Thomas?' he asked.

She shook her head. 'Not since yesterday. He won't come now. Old Baldy's on the watch.'

'I know. I saw him. But he can't sit all afternoon – knitting.'

Lil giggled. 'Ain't he a caution? What's he doin' – knitting hisself a lacey jumper?'

Ben laughed until he almost fell out of the tree. 'I don't think so,' he gasped. 'It was all different colours. A sort of big square.'

' 'E won't stay much after five o'clock,' Lil said.

'How d'you know?'

' 'E'll go 'ome then to see his ole auntie. She's bedridden and he lives wiv her, see? She's got a daughter, too, but she's a barmaid, so she works evenings. Old Baldy goes home 'bout five to give the ole girl tea.'

Ben wondered how she knew this. He must have looked surprised or disbelieving because she went on quickly, 'I know 'cause he lives in our street. Opposite, as a matter of fact. Everyone round us knows Old Baldy.'

Ben remembered something. 'Why did you say you didn't trust him, the other day?'

'Oh – I dunno.' She picked at a piece of loose bark on the tree with her small, bony fingers and looked embarrassed. 'He's just a funny customer. A slyboots, my Mum says.'

'It wasn't anything real – nothing he'd done, I mean?'

She muttered, 'Jus' a feeling. He gives me the willies.'

'Me, too,' Ben agreed, but he felt disappointed. If Lil had had a definite reason for not trusting Old Baldy, he would have had something more concrete to tell Thomas. He settled himself more comfortably on the branch and said, 'Where do you live?'

'What d'you want to know for?'

'I just asked. There's no harm in asking.'

'Well – I live here. I mean this is our garden. That's how I met Thomas, see? Our garden's at the bottom of his.' She paused. 'Only we don't live in the whole of the 'ouse. Mum and me – we've got the basement.'

'And you're there, on your own?'

She nodded. 'I creeps in an' out ever so quiet. It wouldn't do for anyone to hear me, see, 'cause they'd tell the Welfare lady. When I'm in, I feed our budgie and clean up a bit so it'll be all nice for me Mum when she comes home.' She sighed a little. 'It gets a bit lonely, though.'

Ben said, 'Are you hungry – I mean, if you haven't seen Thomas today . . . ?'

'I'm starved,' she said simply, and then blushed, as if it were somehow shameful to be hungry. She went on quickly, 'I've got some money – I mean I've got some in the post office but I can't get it out. If I went to the shops, someone 'ud see me.'

Ben said, 'I could go for you, if you like. I couldn't go to the post office because of signing the form, but I could use my money and go to a shop.'

'I don't want your money,' she said with a deeply insulted air.

Ben said patiently, 'I could lend it to you, until your mother comes back. I've only got about five shillings but you're welcome to borrow it.'

She looked suspiciously at him. 'I'll pay you back. I'm not *takin'* anything. My Mum says . . .'

Ben broke in, 'That's what I meant. What would you like me to buy?'

She half closed her eyes and ran the tip of her pink tongue over her lips. 'Sherbet dab. An' a liquorice pipe, an' a Mars Bar . . .'

It didn't seem a very good diet for a starving person. Ben thought that in her place, he would want something more solid, like sausages and chips. That was an idea. He would buy the sweets and add sixpennyworth of chips. Then on his way back he could get some fruit from his father's flat and a packet of sausages. It was a pity he had eaten all those apples, but there were oranges left and one rather squashy banana. Lil wouldn't mind. She mightn't want to take his money but she didn't seem to have any principles about other people's food.

'I'll be back soon,' he promised, as he slid down the tree.

'Ben,' she called after him urgently. 'Ben . . .'

'Yes?' He looked up. 'What is it?'

'I a'most forgot. Git some bird-seed for our budgie, will you. The kind that's got extra vitamins in it.'

Ben was longer than he had meant to be because after he had been to the shops for the bird-seed and the sweets and searched for a fish-and-chip shop without success, he decided to look at the street where Lil and Old Baldy lived. An alleyway at the end of the terrace led into a street of smaller houses at the back. Once, it had probably been a mews where the servants lived who worked in the big houses – part was still cobbled for the horses' hooves – but now it was a run-down, noisy slum, full of dogs rooting after rubbish in the gutter and children playing hop-scotch while their mothers gossiped on the doorsteps. It was a warm, lively little street, full of sun.

Ben walked slowly along, wondering which house Lil lived in.

In one of the basement windows, a small cage was hanging, carefully placed to get all the sunshine. Inside the cage a budgerigar twittered on its perch. Ben leant over the railings round the area and called softly, 'Joey, Joey . . .' Then he realized that even if the bird knew its name, it could not hear him through the closed window. Ben straightened up, feeling foolish.

Then he remembered Lil had said Old Baldy lived opposite. He glanced curiously across the road and saw a most astonishing sight. At least, it was astonishing in *that* street – a long, shining, yellow Jaguar car parked by the kerb. Ben crossed the road, he couldn't resist it. It was so very shiny, so very new; the blue leather seats inside looked as if no one had ever sat on them. There was a splendid fog lamp in the middle of the front bonnet. The number of the car was PJ5781. Ben murmured it once, and had it by heart. (Ben, who was monumentally lazy at school, could always memorize useless bits of information like other people's car numbers, without effort.)

He was standing on the pavement, admiring his bulbous reflexion in the car's nearside wing, when a sharp tapping sound made him turn round. A young, plump woman in a blue summer dress was banging on the window of the house and making angry faces at him. Presumably, Ben thought, this was her beautiful car. He grinned at her amiably and was about to walk on without resentment – it was understandable, after all, that she should be anxious about this marvellous machine – when he noticed someone beside her, in the window.

An old, old lady was sitting, propped up in a high-backed chair and looking out of the window. She was wrapped in a knitted shawl made of different colours.

A shawl. *That* was what Old Baldy was knitting, Ben thought, and then: perhaps he was knitting it for *her*. This was Old Baldy's auntie, he was quite sure of it. The young woman was her daughter. And the car?

'The Jag belongs to Old Baldy,' Lil said, speaking with difficulty because her mouth was full of Mars Bar. 'S'matter of fact, that's one of the things that's funny about 'im.'

'What d'you mean?'

'Well, it stands to reason, don't it? I mean if a person suddenly comes into the money. An' it's not just the *car*. The things that've gone into that 'ouse this last month! My Mum says it's a wonder they can move about. And since she went into 'ospital they've had a new telly. 'Bout as big as their front room.'

'Perhaps he's won a football pool,' Ben said thoughtfully.

She shook her head. 'He'd have said, wouldn't he? I mean, you tell people. No, there's something funny gone on, as my Mum said. Once she asked 'im. She said – joking like o' course – " 'Ave you come into a fortune, Mr Baldry?" An' *he* said – mind you, he was in a good mood, he in't always so jolly – "No, Mrs Bates, I've jus' bin selling off a few of the family diamonds".'

'I wonder what made him say that?' Ben said.

'Jus' a sort of joke, only telling my Mum to mind her own flipping business . . .' Lil looked at Ben sharply. 'What's the matter? Something on your mind?'

'No . . .' Ben said. In fact, his mind was working feverishly. It might not be a joke, even though Old Baldy had meant it as one. It might just have been the first thing that came into his head – and it had come into his head because it happened to be true. Suppose there was a plot. Suppose Old Baldy was one of the men Uncle Tuku had talked about, who were corrupted by riches? The riches that came from the diamond mines? He said, 'It must be getting on for five o'clock. D'you

think Thomas will come out soon? There's something I want
to talk to him about.'

'What?'

'Well – it's a secret.'

Lil looked daggers at him. 'Keep it to yourself, then. You'll
have to. He won't be coming.'

'How d'you know?'

' 'Cause he *told* me, stupid. I saw him after you'd gone to
the shops. He came to the wall and whistled and said he
couldn't stay 'cause Miss Fisher wanted 'im to have an early
tea 'cause . . .'

'Why didn't you tell me?'

'Didn't ask, did you?'

'No.' Ben felt irritated, though it wasn't really her fault.
'I suppose it'll have to wait till tomorrow,' he said.

'Have to wait longer than *that*.' Lil finished her Mars Bar
and wiped her sticky fingers on her jeans before starting in on
the sherbet dab. 'Won't be 'ere tomorrow, either.' She shot
Ben a triumphant look as she opened the corner of the sherbet
packet.

'*Why?*' Ben almost shouted at her, so that she shrank back,
looking rather frightened. He hadn't meant to frighten her,
but he was feeling rather scared himself.

She said nervously, ' 'Cause he's going away. First thing
tomorrow. 'Is Uncle Joseph's taking 'im away for an 'oliday
in the country, he was ever so excited . . .' She stopped.
'What's the matter? You look ever so pasty . . .'

8

'I AM BETRAYED'

THOMAS'S bedroom was to the left of the fire-escape. Watching from the garden, Ben had seen him, silhouetted against the light, opening the upper half of the sash window.

Ben crept up the fire-escape until he was level with the top floor of the house. By climbing round until he was underneath the iron frame and twisting himself downwards and sideways, clinging to the steps with one hand and steadying himself against a drainpipe with the other, he was able to peer through the window and see Thomas, sitting up in bed and reading. Even for Ben, this was a precarious position and he felt dizzy and slightly sick.

'Thomas,' he whispered, '*Thomas*,' terrified that the boy would cry out.

But though Thomas looked up, startled, there was no sound except the little *thump* of his feet as he got out of bed and came to the window.

'Is that you, Ben?' he said – stupidly, Ben thought, because after all he was looking straight at him – and then, 'What *are* you doing?' He made no move to open the window wider and Ben was suddenly conscious of the awful black drop beneath.

'Enjoying myself, you crazy nit,' he said savagely. Thomas continued to look at him, his jaw hanging open in surprise. Ben's hand, clinging to the fire-escape, was beginning to grow numb; his arm felt as if it were being wrenched from the socket. 'Let me in, stupid. I can't go on and on, hanging here like a sort of mangy *bat*.'

'Sorry,' Thomas said, at once. He dragged a chair over to the window and eased the top half of the window down as far

66

as he could, trying to prevent it rattling in its frame. Ben righted himself cautiously, fastening both hands on to the fire-escape and feeling for the open window with his feet, lowering himself carefully inside. There was a horrible moment when he had to let go his handhold; the ridge of the window was against his thighs and he was afraid he would overbalance and fall headfirst into the garden below. Then Thomas caught at his legs and guided them firmly on to the sill.

Stepping down into the room, Ben drew a long, shaky sigh and rubbed his hands together. They were white and stiffly curled from clinging to the iron steps. Thomas tiptoed to the door, opened it, listened, and shut it again. He turned to Ben and said in a severe, priggish tone, 'You should not have come here. It is not safe.'

'You're telling *me*,' Ben said. Suddenly he felt indignant that Thomas was not more welcoming. After all, he had nearly killed himself coming here! Then he remembered why he had come, and his anger died. He looked at Thomas's worried face and said, 'I didn't come just for fun. I came to tell you something important.'

They sat on Thomas's bed. Ben told him everything. As he had suspected, it sounded not exactly silly, but rather as if he had been exaggerating something quite simple and easily explained in order to make himself important.

It seemed clear that Thomas felt this, or something like this, anyway, though he was too polite to say so.

He said, 'But my Uncle Joseph is only going to take me out of London, into the country. I do not think there is anything dangerous in that. I am quite safe, and my father is quite safe, as long as I stay in England. Uncle Tuku has explained to me.'

'It *sounds* all right. But why should Uncle Joseph act so funny then? Like a sort of spy? I mean if it's all right for you to go, safe and that, why doesn't he want to tell Uncle Tuku? Why does he want to sort of *sneak* you away?'

Thomas looked puzzled. 'I think – I think Uncle Joseph is

a little afraid of Uncle Tuku. Uncle Tuku treats him like a child. I think perhaps Uncle Joseph did not want to discuss his plan with Uncle Tuku in case he said no. It would humiliate Uncle Joseph, you see . . .'

Ben said doggedly, 'I still think he's going to a lot of – well – *trouble*. Are you sure there isn't any chance that he's – he's *against* you?'

Thomas screwed up his eyes, assessing the situation gravely. 'I know there is some quarrel between my uncles, but sometimes families do quarrel. It does not mean they will betray each other.' He hesitated. 'Uncle Tuku does not always trust Uncle Joseph. That is because he is often foolish and excitable. But Uncle Joseph is my mother's younger brother. I cannot believe that he would want to harm us. Though' – Thomas's eyes widened and he looked suddenly fearful – 'though it *was* Uncle Joseph who wanted my father to stay in Tiga. And . . .'

Ben broke in excitedly, 'Perhaps he wanted your father to be caught. Perhaps someone has bribed him to kidnap you so your father will have to go back to Tiga . . .'

The alarmed look faded from Thomas's eyes and he shook his head scornfully. 'My Uncle Joseph is rich. My mother's family were rich and powerful when my father was a poor boy at a mission school. They were once the great Chiefs of Tiga.' He sat up, very straight and proud, looking rather like a young Chief himself. 'So you see, Ben, my Uncle Joseph could not be *bribed*.' He shrugged his shoulders. 'Old Baldy could be bribed, perhaps Miss Fisher too. She must be a very poor woman, or she would not have to work, now she is old. I think you must be wrong, Ben. It is just a sort of game of my Uncle Joseph's. He wants to take me out of London to – to tease my Uncle Tuku. Perhaps he wants to frighten him a little.' He gave a deep sigh. 'I wish I could understand. It sounds strange – but what can I do? I cannot disobey my Uncle Joseph.'

'You could tell Uncle Tuku.' Ben wondered why he had

not thought of this before. He noticed that Thomas was looking at him rather oddly, but he was so relieved to have found
such an easy solution that he went on cheerfully, 'I mean,
Uncle Joseph hasn't asked *you* not to, has he? I know you
shouldn't give people away, but sometimes, in important
things, you have to. It's not just telling tales . . .'

'But Uncle Tuku is not here,' Thomas said. 'He has flown
home to Tiga.'

Ben felt his heart flutter up into his throat. This was really
bad . . . Somehow, though Uncle Tuku was terrifying, Ben
knew that he was a safe, dependable person. And at the back
of his mind, all the time he had been trying to frighten himself
about Uncle Joseph and his plotting, he had known that while
Uncle Tuku was there, nothing dreadful could really happen
to Thomas. But now . . .

He said frantically, 'But he *can't*. I mean he can't have gone
– it'll be too dangerous for him in Tiga.'

'Uncle Tuku is not afraid of danger,' Thomas said proudly,
holding his head very high. And then, more sensibly, Ben
thought. 'But he will be safe. He has never really been in
politics, you see, he has only advised my father. And he is old
and important. Nogola might want to harm him but he would
not dare.'

'What has he gone back *for*?' Ben asked, dismayed.

'I don't know. I think . . .' Thomas began and then stopped
and sat, listening.

Ben listened too. He heard a flip-flapping sound as if someone was coming up the stairs in a pair of old, loose slippers.

For a full minute, the boys looked at each other, speechless
with horror.

Ben bolted under the bed, like a rabbit into the burrow, just
before the door opened.

The bed was just high enough for him to lie flat and the
covers lapped over and concealed him. Edging aside a fold of
blanket, he could see Miss Fisher's feet in a pair of red slippers

with fluffy pom-poms on the toes and part of her curiously straight legs, as fat at the ankles as they were higher up, in fawn wool stockings. The feet moved towards the bed and stopped a few inches from Ben's nose.

Miss Fisher said, 'Still reading, Thomas? You'll tire your eyes. And do you like sleeping with your window as wide open as that? Won't you catch cold?' She didn't wait for an answer but went on, rather nervously Ben thought – though why should she be nervous of a boy? – 'I just thought I ought to come up and see you were all right.' A pause. 'You are all right, aren't you, Thomas?'

Thomas said in a sleepy-sounding voice, 'Yes, Miss Fisher.'

'Good. I just thought I'd see . . .' The feet seemed to hesitate, then they changed position and the bed springs creaked as she sat down on the side of the bed.

There was a silence that seemed to last an uncomfortably long time. It was dusty under the bed and Ben felt his nostrils begin to tickle. Then Miss Fisher said in that same, odd, nervous tone, 'You do like your Uncle Joseph, don't you, dear?'

'Yes,' Thomas said.

Ben's left leg was getting cramp. He moved it and jarred his foot against one of the bed castors. At once the bed began to bump a little as if Thomas had heard the sound and was moving about to distract Miss Fisher's attention.

'Aren't you comfortable?' she said, and then, coaxingly, 'You will enjoy a little holiday with Uncle Joseph, won't you? It'll be nice to be out of stuffy old London and be free to – er – run about and enjoy the beauties of Nature, won't it?'

'Aren't you coming with us?' was all Thomas said.

'I – I'm afraid not,' Miss Fisher cleared her throat. 'I've found I've got to go away for a little. My sister's not well.'

The bed was suddenly very still.

Miss Fisher went on, 'When your Uncle Tuku comes back I want you to tell him something from me. Tell him that I did what I thought was best for you.'

'He said you were going to stay with me,' Thomas said. 'I – I *want* you to, Miss Fisher.'

'Do you?' Her voice changed and she gave a flustered, pleased little laugh. 'Well, that's a nice surprise! I didn't think you'd want funny old Fisher. Of course, I've always had a knack with young people but somehow I didn't think you and I had *quite* hit it off.'

'Please don't leave me, Miss Fisher,' Thomas said.

'Oh, dear,' Miss Fisher said. 'Oh, dear.' She gave a little sigh. The bed springs creaked, probably, Ben thought, because she had moved nearer to Thomas, to comfort him. 'I really am sorry,' she said. 'I would like to stay, if I could. If I'd known you'd mind so much ...' Her voice trailed off indecisively. She was silent for a moment and then said firmly, 'You'll be all right, Thomas. I'm sure your uncle will take good care of you and I expect you'll find he isn't as fussy as I am about keeping clean and eating too many ice-creams and things like that!' She was speaking brightly now, in the silly way some people speak to children when they have to do something unpleasant, like taking medicine or going back to school.

Thomas said nothing.

'Funny little boy,' Miss Fisher said tenderly. 'I'll say good-night now, and you can go to sleepy-byes.' The bed shot up as she got off it. Her feet moved a little way, into the middle of the room, then they stopped. She said, 'Thomas – just one thing. Were you sick, when you came here in the plane?'

'A bit,' Thomas said. 'It was an exceptionally bumpy flight.'

'Oh,' Miss Fisher said. 'That's a pity.' Then she went on in a very low voice as if she were afraid of being overheard, 'Listen, dear. I – I shouldn't be telling you this, I mean it was meant as a surprise, but your uncle might – just *might* be giving you an extra special treat. He's thinking of taking you to Scotland, in an aeroplane.' Her voice was shaky now, almost frightened, Ben thought. 'He told me not to tell you, but I can't bear to think you might be ill. I've got some special pills.

I'll give them to you tomorrow, before you go. Then you won't be sick on the plane.'

There was a long pause. 'Thank you, Miss Fisher,' Thomas said.

'You won't tell your uncle, will you? He'd be so upset because I've spoiled his surprise. You wouldn't want to get poor Miss Fisher into trouble.'

'No,' Thomas said. 'I won't tell him, Miss Fisher.'

The door closed. Her feet flapped down the stairs. Ben wriggled out of his hiding-place. Thomas was out of bed and standing in the middle of the room.

'I am betrayed,' he said. His eyes were very bright. 'Poor Miss Fisher. She does not understand. Once he gets me to the airport, he will take me back to Tiga.'

'You said Uncle Joseph would never betray you.' Though he was very excited, Ben felt bound to point this out.

'Not for money.'

'Then why?'

'I don't know. I don't understand. But I can't trust him now.' Thomas looked suddenly much younger, small and frightened. 'What can I do?'

'You'll have to escape,' Ben said.

'Where to? Oh, *Ben*.' Thomas's eyes blazed. 'We will escape together. Into the mountains.'

'There aren't any mountains near London.'

'Into the bush, then.'

'There isn't any bush, either,' Ben said. It was difficult to explain what England was like to someone who had always lived in Africa. 'I mean, there's only country near London and even the country's stuffed full of houses and people. England's awfully small. There aren't any real lonely places, not where you could hide.'

Thomas frowned for a moment and then said, in a lordly way, 'I will leave it to you, Ben. It is your country.'

Ben was thinking. When you were hiding from someone,

the best thing was often to find a place quite near, almost under their noses. 'We could go to Lil's,' he said. 'It would do for a start. I can get food so you won't starve.' He stopped. 'How long will you need to escape *for*, do you think?'

'Till my father is safe, in America. Or until Uncle Tuku comes back.' Suddenly Thomas grinned, an enormous, happy grin. 'It will be *lovely*, Ben,' he said fervently. He began to pull off his pyjamas and scramble into his clothes as if this whole business was a game invented for his amusement. Ben frowned. Though he could feel the same excitement, tingling through his whole body like a massive attack of pins and needles, he reminded himself that this was serious. He looked at Thomas who was getting into his white silk shirt, his long white socks. 'Haven't you any other clothes?'

Thomas stood on one leg. 'Lots. But they're in the wardrobe in Miss Fisher's room. We could steal in and get them, if you like. We could pretend to be robbers.' He gave a high, excited laugh.

Ben frowned even more fiercely. If Thomas was going to behave like this, he could see he would have to be serious for both of them. '*Ssh*,' he whispered. 'We won't do that . . .' He stole to the door and opened it an inch. The landing outside was in darkness. It was very quiet except for the plop, plop of a dripping tap. He said, 'Can we get on to the fire-escape through the bathroom?'

Thomas nodded. 'The window sticks, though.'

'If we both push, I expect we can move it. *Hurry*.'

Thomas led the way across the black landing to the bathroom. The window was high in the wall, but by standing close together on the lavatory seat, they managed to move it upwards, slowly and jerkily. A little breeze blew in from the gardens. They could hear the trees stir. 'You first,' Ben said. He helped Thomas through the window and heard the scrape of his feet on the fire-escape. Then Thomas's face appeared at the window. He whispered, 'I haven't got my toothbrush.'

Ben, who never cleaned his teeth – or his fingernails, or his ears – if he could possibly avoid it, stared at Thomas blankly. So blankly, that Thomas imagined toothbrushes must be unknown in England. He explained. 'It's a sort of plastic stick with a tiny brush on the end. You use it night and morning. For the teeth,' he added helpfully. When Ben continued to look at him with astonishment, he craned his neck in through the window. 'Over there. Mine's the red one. Next to Miss Fisher's. Hers is green.'

Like someone in a trance, Ben took the red toothbrush out of the chromium-plated holder and handed it to Thomas. Thomas took it.

'Thank you. Miss Fisher would be so cross if I went to bed without cleaning my teeth.'

Ben began to giggle. He couldn't help it. The idea – the very idea of a fugitive from danger, terrible danger, perhaps, stopping to collect an old toothbrush! 'Sure you don't want your flannel too?' he gasped, and laughed so much that he overbalanced and had to clutch at the lavatory chain to stop himself falling.

The cistern emptied with a dreadful noise. It was like standing under Niagara Falls.

Thomas danced up and down on the fire-escape. 'What are you doing, Ben?' he said. 'They'll *hear*.'

Ben drew a deep breath and heaved himself up, lying across the window-sill. He wriggled round so that he could drop feet first on to the iron staircase. He was wearing a new belt his father had bought him the other day; a fine belt with a special ring to attach his penknife to. The belt caught on the sill. Ben tugged at it, suddenly panic-stricken. Someone *had* heard. A voice – Miss Fisher's – was calling 'Thomas, Thomas . . .'

'Oh, hell,' Ben said. 'Oh, *hell*,' and wrenched himself free. 'I've broken my belt,' he moaned, clutching the ends around him.

'Don't worry about your old *belt*. Not *now*,' Thomas said.

They threw caution to the winds and ran down the fire-escape, noisy as a herd of elephants doing their level best to waken the dead. They flew across the garden to the wall. As they reached it, Ben stumbled over something soft that streaked like a shadow between his legs. A frightful sound rose and shattered the quiet of the night.

'Thomas,' Ben shouted in terror, and Thomas answered from the top of the wall.

'Hurry, Ben, they'll catch us . . .'

But Miss Fisher and Uncle Joseph were too late. When they got to the bathroom and looked out of the window, there was nothing and nobody to be seen.

Only the wind and the trees, and a thin, stray cat miauling like a banshee on the garden wall.

9

LIL AND JOEY

THEY were lying on the other side of the wall, flat on the moist earth. After the cat had stopped screeching – a terrible sound that froze the marrow of their bones – Uncle Joseph had come into the garden and called, 'Thomas, Thomas,' but very softly as if he were unwilling to arouse the neighbourhood. Now he had gone indoors – they had heard his steps on the iron stair – and there was no sound at all except the pounding of their own, fearful hearts.

Thomas whispered, 'What will happen if they catch us, Ben?'

'Shut up. Lie still,' Ben whispered back, not because he thought anyone could hear their voices, but because he didn't know the answer to Thomas's question and he didn't want to think about it just yet. Like most people in that kind of situation, he sounded angry. He was discovering an awkward truth: that there is a world of difference between planning to do something and actually doing it. In Thomas's bedroom it had seemed not only exciting to escape, but the most natural thing to do. Lying on the ground, in the dark and the silence, a hollow pit of fear opened up in front of him. If Uncle Joseph caught them, what would he do? Not only to Thomas, but to *him*. Ben closed his eyes and squeezed them tight as if he could shut out this terrible thought. What had he done? He had poked his nose into something that wasn't his business at all. And not only that. He didn't really understand what it was that he had poked his nose into! What did he know about Uncle Joseph and Uncle Tuku? Perhaps Uncle Joseph was a good man who wished Thomas no harm . . . He should never have persuaded Thomas to run away. Politics were for grown people, not for boys. And he was only a boy. He began to feel sorry for himself. If he hadn't interfered, he would be lying safe between cool sheets, on a soft pillow, with the dark night safely shut outside the window. Although Ben usually hated going to sleep – it was such a waste of time – he found himself thinking of his bed with a kind of yearning that was almost like homesickness. He was on the edge of tears.

Beside him, Thomas was obediently silent. He had wriggled close to Ben for comfort. But after a little, he decided that the silence was more awful than Ben's disapproval. He said, 'What are we going to do? I'm so – so cold.'

He meant 'frightened', Ben knew. And knowing Thomas was frightened, stiffened Ben's pride. He had been wondering whether it wouldn't be best to abandon the whole thing and tell Thomas that he must go back. Instead, he said with a show of cheerfulness, ' 'Course you're not. On a night like this! It's just nerves.' All the same, he could feel that Thomas was shivering, trembling all over like a wet dog. Ben felt for his hand. 'Don't worry. I'll fix everything,' he said softly. 'Come on, now. We're going to find Lil.'

He led the way cautiously down the garden. It smelt of dust-bins, rotten vegetables and cats. They came to the house and stood at the top of the stone steps that led down to the area. The basement window was dark.

'Is this where she lives?' Thomas said.

'I hope so. Wait here.'

He crept down the steps. The smell of cats was very strong. The window was barred. He put his hand through the bars and tapped on the window.

Thomas had followed him like a shadow. 'She won't answer. Not a knock. Only if I do our special whistle.'

' Make it good and soft, then.'

Thomas pursed his lips. The noise that came out was liquid, warbling and rather eerie, like the cry of some strange bird. Ben had never heard a whistle like this; he could make a mar-vellous, screeching sound with both fingers in his mouth, but never, never a sound like this. He forgot the purpose of the whistle in his envy and admiration so that it was almost a sur-prise when a door at the side of the area creaked open.

Lil's small face peered through the crack, white and startled.

'It's all right,' Ben said quickly, sorry if they had startled her. 'It's only us.'

But sympathy was wasted on Lil. 'I've got eyes, haven't I?' she said tartly. She creaked the door wider. 'What are you playin' at?'

'Tell you inside.' Ben propelled Thomas in front of him. Lil shut the door. They stood in a pitch-dark hole, like a cell.

'Wait on,' Lil said. A door opened in the cell, into a tiny room that was dimly lit by a table lamp with a red cloth thrown over the shade. The lamp stood on a wooden chair pushed close to a narrow bed against the wall. The only other furni-ture was a chest of drawers. The floor was bare, splintery boards; the walls were a muddy, yellowish colour except in one place, just above the bed, where the plaster had fallen off and the grey laths showed through. The sheets on the bed were tumbled open but Lil was still wearing her jeans and old jersey. Did she sleep in them, Ben wondered? Fancy having no one to see you got undressed before you went to bed, no one to make you brush your teeth or wash behind your ears! He looked at Lil with envy.

She was staring at them, the pupils of her eyes enlarged and dark in her pale face. Suddenly, she flushed up and said, 'You oughter see the front room. We've fixed it up lovely. We was going to do this one when Mum had her accident. Though o' course there's not much point doin' much in a rented place. Jus' money down the drain, Mum says.'

'I think it's a nice room,' Ben said sincerely. 'Cosy.'

Lil was looking round her in a troubled way, like Aunt Mabel when she was wondering if she could afford new curtains and covers. 'One day we're goin' to buy a little house and I'm goin' to have a bedroom with roses on the wallpaper and curtains to match and a pink carpet. Mum's got it all worked out.' She glared at Ben, as if she thought he might disbelieve her. ' 'Course, it'll be a good, big room. Not like this. Mum says there isn't room to swing a cat here.'

'Have you got a cat?' Thomas asked in a puzzled voice.

The stiff, defiant look faded from Lil's face. ' 'Course not. It's just something you say.' Her eyes fell upon Ben's knee and she gave a little gasp. '*What* have you bin and gone and done?' she said accusingly, and for the second time, Ben was reminded of Aunt Mabel. All women were alike, he thought resignedly, and looked down at his knee. It was covered in blood; the tops of his long, grey socks were stiff with it. He supposed he must have cut himself on the glass when he scrambled over the wall. The curious thing was that until this minute it hadn't hurt him at all; now, as he looked down, the knee began to throb and burn and he felt quite dizzy with the pain of it. 'Oh, that's nothing,' he said.

'Let me see,' Lil said imperiously. She took the lamp off the chair and motioned Ben to sit down. Then she knelt in front of him, the lamp in her hand, her small face serious and intent. 'Can't really see. It's full of muck and dirt.' She prodded with a grubby forefinger and Ben winced. 'It's got a bit of glass in it.'

'It's all right – don't *fuss*,' Ben said impatiently, jerking his knee away. 'What's worse is that I broke my new belt. Dad'll be *mad*.' He pulled it out of his pocket where he had stuffed it as he ran across the garden and saw, at once, that something much worse had happened than a mere broken belt. 'My penknife's gone,' he said. 'The ring must have broken off.'

'Never mind about your old penknife,' Lil said. She had hold of his knee. 'You've got to get this glass splinter out or it'll go *inward*.' She sat back on her heels, her face solemn. 'An' once it's got in, it travels round and round inside you till it gets to the heart. Then,' she put her hand on her chest, 'then, it *pierces you dead*.'

There was something horribly convincing about the way she said this. Ben forgot about his penknife.

Thomas said, 'Oh, Ben, we must get a doctor.'

Lil shook her head. 'I 'spect it's too late. It'll have got in already. Can't you *feel* it?' She looked at Ben thoughtfully, her head on one side. 'Working its way into your *veins*. It happened to my Granny once. She was a dressmaker, see, and she used to poke the needles in her blouse when she was working. One day she poked too hard an' the needle went *in*. She was lucky, though. It worked all round her and come out through her big toe.'

Ben could feel it. The wicked little piece of glass was travelling inside him, moving, the way a burr will move inside your clothes. There was a nasty pricking sensation in his leg.

'How long does it take?' he whispered.

'Jus' a few minutes sometimes,' Lil said in a hollow voice.

The two boys looked at her. Ben was white as paper. Tears stood in Thomas's big, brown eyes.

Then Lil's face began to twitch. To their horror, she began to laugh, her small hand in front of her mouth, her shoulders shaking. She said, between gasps, 'That took you in, din't it?'

Ben was too relieved to be angry. 'Isn't it true, then?' he said in a faint voice.

She shook her head. 'Jus' old wives tale,' she said scornfully. 'But it oughter be seen to. Germs. You hold this.' She thrust the lamp at Thomas and went out of the room. They heard the spurt of a tap. Then she came back, carrying a basin and a towel. Her sleeves were rolled up. 'I've washed me 'ands,' she said, and plumped down in front of Ben. 'Hold the light still, Tommy boy.'

She began to sponge Ben's knee. Her small hands were gentle. She worked slowly and methodically, the tip of her pink tongue sticking out of the side of her mouth. Girls were funny, Ben thought. Like kittens; spit and scratch one minute and all purrs and softness the next.

'I think it's all right,' she said finally. 'It oughter have disinfectant. But I haven't got none.' She dried her hands on the towel and looked up at them both. She said, in a surprised voice as if this had only just occurred to her, 'You haven't told me what you come for.'

'I've run away from my uncle,' Thomas said. 'Ben said it was the best thing. He said I could come and hide here, with you.'

'Has he bin knocking you about?' she said, with interest.

'Of course not.' Thomas looked astonished. 'It is just that it is not safe to stay with him any more.'

'Why?'

'I – I can't tell you.'

'Why?' She smiled coaxingly. 'C'm on. Tell me the big secret.'

'It's a matter of politics,' Thomas said, politely but firmly.

'You wouldn't understand. Women do not understand politics.'

Ben sighed. He could have told Thomas that it was no earthly good taking this grand, masculine line with Lil. Her mouth set mulishly. She stood up, holding the towel and basin.

'All right. Keep your precious secret, Clever Dick,' she said. 'An' run along home. I've got better things to do than play games with a pair of nutty kids.'

Thomas and Ben looked at each other in dismay. Everything depended on Lil. If Thomas couldn't stay here, with her, they had no other plan . . .

Thomas said, 'Lil, I'm sorry if I have offended you. I didn't mean . . .'

'Get lost,' she said, and stuck her nose in the air.

'Listen, Lil,' Ben said quickly. 'It isn't a game. His uncle wants to take him back to Africa.'

'Africa's his country, ain't it?' She stood still, her back turned on them both, her head proud and high.

'But he doesn't want to go – they're going to *kidnap* him.'

'So I should care?'

Ben felt desperate. 'If they do, something dreadful might happen. He might be put in prison.' Thomas opened his mouth but Ben signed to him to keep quiet. His imagination took wings. 'Thrown into a dreadful, dark jail like – like a *criminal*. It's a wicked plot. Uncle Joseph's in it, and Old Baldy. He . . .'

'*Old Baldy?*' Lil said in a strangled voice.

'Yes. You know you said you didn't trust him . . .'

She whirled round to face them, dropping the basin on the floor. The water splashed over their feet. 'D'you mean Thomas might be put in prison along of Old Baldy?' To their astonishment the tears were streaming down her face. 'Why didn't you say so before?' she sobbed. 'I'd do anything – I jus' hate Old Baldy . . .'

'Then Thomas can stay? He can hide here?' Ben said eagerly.

She nodded and sniffed, wiping her eyes with the back of her hand. She said, to Thomas, 'You c'n sleep in the front room, so long as you don't mess it up. It's all tidy, ready for me Mum.'

'I'll be very careful,' Thomas said.

'You can't have a light. Someone 'ud see. And you gotta be quiet. Or someone'll know I'm here and they'll tell the Welfare . . .'

'I will be quiet, too.' Thomas went up to her and took her hand. 'Are we friends now, Lil?'

The tears welled up again. She turned her head away as if she were ashamed of them. 'It was you forgot we was friends, not me,' she said. Then, with a spurt of anger, 'I jus' hate boys who keep secrets from girls. As if girls weren't good enough to be told things. Some boys go on as if girls weren't ornery people – s'if they weren't even 'uman.'

'I'm sorry, Lil,' Thomas said. 'I was stupid. Please accept my apology.'

She looked at him. 'All right,' she said awkwardly.

'And if you like I will explain it all to you. About the revolution in my country and the general situation. Tiga has a most interesting history . . .'

Lil gave a delicate little yawn. 'Sounds a bit boring,' she said. 'Tell you what! I'll show you our Joey.'

The boys followed her to the door of the front room. That was all there was to the flat, two tiny rooms and a kitchen. The front room smelt of polish. 'Pine Tar,' Lil said, wrinkling her nose appreciatively. 'That's what Mum likes. I've given it a real good goin' over.'

The light from the street lamp outside the window showed them a few, dim shapes of furniture and the bird-cage, hanging in the window. As Lil unhooked it, there was a muffled cheep.

Back in her small room, she removed the cage cover and a sleepy bird, fluffed up on his perch like a knitted ball, stretched his blue neck and regarded them with pin-point eyes. Lil took him out and held him gently against her cheek. 'Only thing is, he don't talk yet. One day Mum says she'll git us a bird that talks. S'not that he ain't intelligent, though. He's intelligent all right. Mum says he knows everything, that bird.'

'You ought to ask your father to bring you home a parrot,' Ben said. 'I thought all sailors had parrots.'

She gave him a side-long look. Then she said hastily, 'Oh, he's had hundreds. But he's going to bring me better things than an old parrot. Next time, he's goin' to bring me an alligator. An' – an' a baby gorilla.'

'They're very difficult to look after,' Ben said.

'Not for my Dad. He's a wonder with animals, my Dad.'

'I once had a lion cub,' Thomas said. 'Only he grew too big. Can I hold your bird, Lil?'

'He might not take to you. He's particular wiv strangers.'

At this, Joey gave a little squawk, stretched his wings and fluttered out of Lil's hand to land on Thomas's shoulder where he sat, preening himself. 'See what I mean?' Lil cried with delight. 'He understands every word we say. He's taken a real fancy to you.'

Thomas smiled. It seemed to split his face in two.

'He is a most beautiful bird,' he said. 'I wonder if we could teach him to tell the time? My mother's uncle once had a bird who could do that. He would look at a clock and cry, once for every hour . . .'

Ben looked at the cheap alarm clock on the chest of drawers. To his horror, it said half past ten. His father and Miss Mackingtosh had gone to the pictures. He had promised he would be in bed by nine-thirty. And they would be home any minute now . . .

'I've got to go,' he said.

The two children turned from their happy contemplation of the budgie, and looked surprised.

'Not yet, Ben. Please don't go yet,' Thomas said.

'I must. I'll come back in the morning and we'll have to think of a plan . . .' *What* plan, he thought.

'What are we going to do, Ben?' Thomas asked. He sounded interested, not anxious. Of course, Ben thought with an inward sigh, he had said he would fix everything. But how?

'I'll think of something,' he said.

10

THE LOST PENKNIFE

As he made his way home through the dark gardens, his responsibility lay heavily on Ben's mind. What were they going to do tomorrow? The bravado with which he had promised to 'think of something' faded away and the doubts that had beset him when they lay, hiding from Uncle Joseph behind the wall, returned and grew. To run away yourself was one thing; to persuade someone else to run away, particularly when you didn't altogether understand what they were running away from, was quite another. He ought, as Aunt Mabel would certainly have told him if she had been here, to have known better. He began to wish she *were* here, with her sharp, loving tongue and crisp common sense. Or, at least, that Mary and John were here. Although they had been terribly boring lately – since John had taken to writing poetry and Mary to fussing over her hair – they could always be relied on, at a pinch, to help him out of trouble. This was the first time in his life, he realized, that he had been really on his own. As he dropped from the wall into his own garden, he actually groaned aloud . . .

There was a light on in the flat. Dad was home. Dad . . .

All at once, instead of feeling nervous as he might have

expected to do since he was out so late, he had a blinding sense of relief. Dad knew all about Africa and about politics. He would understand, far better than Aunt Mabel or Mary or John, about Thomas and the Uncles. If Thomas needed protecting, Dad would know the best way to do it. He could trust Dad. Thomas was bound to trust him too.

Ben bounded up the stairs with a light heart.

But when he opened the flat door, his father did not look at all understanding or trusting.

'And where have you been?' he said angrily. He was angry, in the black, unreasonable way of a man who has been badly frightened. The film had been dull, the dullest film he had ever seen and he and Miss Mackingtosh had left long before it ended. They had been back in the flat, waiting and worrying, for more than two hours.

'Just out.' Ben smiled as cheerfully as he could. 'I'm terribly sorry I'm so frightfully late.'

Mr Mallory ignored this graceful apology. His expression remained grim and glowering.

'You promised me you would be in bed by half past nine.'

Behind him, Miss Mackingtosh sat on the sofa, her eyes fixed on the ground. She seemed to be huddling herself up small, as if to pretend she wasn't really there.

'I trusted you,' Mr Mallory said. 'I trusted you to keep your promise and this is how you behave. Sneaking home at this hour! I'm ashamed of you.'

Ben stared at the carpet. It was patterned in green and yellow and a bright, electric blue. It was the ugliest carpet he had ever seen.

'What were you doing?'

Ben said nothing.

'Answer me this minute,' Mr Mallory thundered in a loud, hectoring voice.

'Nothing.' Ben looked at his father, deliberately un-focusing his eyes so that all he saw was a looming, dark shape, outlined with feathery spikes of light. He felt bitter and sullen. He would have had to have done something really ghastly – stolen the Crown Jewels at least – to have deserved a scene like this. He wondered what his father would say if he had stolen the Crown Jewels, and a snigger escaped him.

'Don't be insolent,' his father said.

'Oh, look – he's hurt his poor knee,' Miss Mackingtosh said in a humble voice. A nervous smile twitched the corners of her mouth as if she were trying to placate Mr Mallory and reassure Ben at the same time.

But Ben's cheeks just burned. 'S'nothing,' he muttered.

'Nothing – nothing, is that the only word in your vocabulary?' Mr Mallory sighed. 'Let's have a look. It's quite clean, Shirley.' He looked at Ben more closely. 'Where's your new belt?'

'Broken,' Ben said. He took it out of his pocket and laid it on the table.

'Hmm,' Mr Mallory said. 'You seem to have made quite an interesting mess of yourself, *doing nothing*. Shirt torn to ribbons, belt broken – quite an achievement for a boy who's been so innocently employed!'

There was a sarcastic edge to his voice that was worse than anger. Ben wished the earth would open and swallow him.

'I've lost my penknife too,' he said, and, to his shame, burst into tears.

Miss Mackingtosh made an unhappy, clicking sound with her tongue. 'Tch, Tch . . .'

Mr Mallory said, a shade – but only a shade – more gently, 'The knife John gave you for your birthday? That's careless, isn't it? Where did you lose it?'

'I – I don't know.'

When had he lost it? Probably when he stuffed his belt into his pocket. His beautiful penknife! He would never dare climb back into Thomas's garden to look for it. It would lie there for ever, hidden under the leaves and the dirt, its bright blades rusting. His sobs increased.

His father said, half sorry, half exasperated, 'You're tired out, that's the trouble. No wonder at this hour. You'd better get along to bed.'

Ben got along. He undressed in a gloomy, desperate mood. He hated himself for his shameful tears. He hated his father. To think he had thought of making him a fellow conspirator, of asking his advice. That hateful man! How unfair of him to go for him like that in front of Miss Mackingtosh – though it was in her favour that she had looked thoroughly uncomfortable as if she had thought it unfair too. But she hadn't said so, had she? She hadn't spoken up for him. She was on his father's side. All grown-ups were on the same side; his father, Miss Mackingtosh, Uncle Joseph – and the Welfare Officer who wanted to take poor Lil away from her own home. As if Lil couldn't look after herself! It was a wonder all children didn't run away. Since they were treated like fools and criminals, why shouldn't they run away and live like outlaws? They could make their own laws – and they would be a good deal better than the ones their parents forced upon them.

These thoughts soothed him considerably. He got into bed and closed his eyes. When his father came in, ten minutes later, he was fast asleep and breathing through his mouth. He was clasping Pin in his hand, for comfort.

Mr Mallory picked up the torn shirt, the blood-stained socks, and stood, looking down at his son. 'Must get something done about those adenoids,' he muttered. There were tear-stains on Ben's cheek. Seeing them, his father gave a deep sigh and bent over the bed. His moustache scraped Ben's skin, but he didn't wake.

Ben slept deeply and soundly, like any good, innocent person with nothing on his mind. He woke later than usual. The sun was already high, the sky blue and promising. Ben lay, blinking and lazy, idly stroking Pin whom he had discovered on the pillow beside his cheek. He lifted the little horse up and watched the sun turn him milky. He stroked the beautiful pricked ears and lapsed into a marvellous daydream in which he and Pin were the same size and could go riding across the sky together.

Then he remembered that it was the beginning of term and thought of all those children who were beginning another long imprisonment with comfortable pity. There would be at least ten more days before John and Mary would be safely out of quarantine. Ten more glorious idyllic days with nothing to do . . .

His heart gave a lurch. There was something he had to do. How could he have forgotten?

The day did not look so nice, after all. Even the fate of all those unfortunate children, setting off for another term's captivity, suddenly seemed more attractive than it had done a minute or two before. At least they *knew* what they had to do. They only had to go to school and suffer the usual round of boredom and stupidity; they didn't have to decide anything important. And, with a bit of luck, there would be an outbreak of mumps or chicken-pox to give them a breathing space of a week or two . . .

Ben never minded being ill during the school term. He began to wonder if he didn't feel a little ill now. Surely his leg was still throbbing? Suppose it was poisoned, and the poison was running through his body? Once, when he had refused to let Aunt Mabel bathe a grazed shin, she had told him a story about a sailor she knew who had neglected a cut on his knee: in the end, his whole leg had been amputated. Ben could feel his leg beginning to ache. He lay still and gave a little groan, which made him feel slightly better. Then, very tenderly, he pushed back the bedclothes and examined his wound. It was healing nicely. Even Aunt Mabel, who was a fuss-pot, wouldn't give it a second look.

He groaned again and got out of bed. His clothes were gone; his leather belt laid out on the chest of drawers. He noticed, without much surprise, because he was used to things being done for him, that it had been clumsily mended. He took clean jeans out of the drawer and began to dress slowly: blue jeans, Tee shirt and an old red sweater Aunt Mabel had knitted for him.

He was lacing up his shoes when he heard something – or someone, rather: a man's voice – not his father's – in the next room. He crept to the door and listened.

His father said, 'I'm sorry, but I really don't think I can help you.'

The other man said something, but very low so that Ben couldn't hear what he said. Although he couldn't remember where or when, he thought he had heard that voice before. He wondered who it belonged to but only distantly; his mind was occupied with a more urgent matter. He needed to go to the bathroom and the way to the bathroom lay through the living-room. And he hadn't wanted to face his father, not just yet, and certainly not when there was another person there.

The need became pressing. Ben sighed and opened the door.

Uncle Joseph was sitting in a chair, facing him.

It took all Ben's courage not to run. He tried the trick of un-focusing his eyes, but it didn't help. Even if he closed them altogether, Uncle Joseph would still be there.

There was only one thing to do, and Ben did it. He marched boldly into the room, keeping his eyes modestly lowered and smiling vaguely but politely as he always did when his father was entertaining business friends who would not want to be bothered with him. He was half-way across the room when his father said, 'My son can tell you himself. Ben, do you know an African boy called Thomas Okapi?'

'No, Dad,' Ben said.

'You're sure you haven't played with him at any time?'

Ben looked straight at him. 'I haven't played with anyone,'

he said. 'I haven't any friends to play with in London.' He was rather pleased with the pathos of this remark. Emboldened, he went on righteously, 'I haven't done anything except walk in the Park, by myself, and go to picture galleries and things.'

His father looked at him thoughtfully for a moment. Then he turned to Uncle Joseph. 'You see? I'm sorry, but I was sure Ben had nothing to do with your nephew's disappearance. I'm afraid I can only advise you to go to the police.'

Uncle Joseph wagged his woolly head sadly. 'It may come to that. Though I am unwilling to call in the police just yet. The matter might get into the papers and, as I am sure you will understand, I do not want to worry my dear sister or my brother-in-law unnecessarily.' He sighed, and went on with what seemed disarming honesty, 'And to tell you the truth, I am deeply ashamed of my own negligence. My dear little nephew was entrusted to me. He was my charge. I do not want his parents to know how badly I have let them down.' He sighed again, more deeply. 'I had hoped, when I came here this morning, that it was just some boyish prank – the kind of thing you and I, Mr Mallory, could easily understand and forgive. Why – we were once boys ourselves! But now your son cannot help me, I am afraid something much more serious may have happened. I tell you, I do not know where to turn! Unless, perhaps, I insert an advertisement in the newspapers. What do you think of that? I would be happy to offer a substantial reward to anyone who could help me to find my dear little nephew.'

Although he was speaking to Mr Mallory, he was looking at Ben. His voice was soft and coaxing but his eyes were sharp: Ben felt as if they were boring right into him. He was caught, like a moth on a pin. He did not want to give Thomas away but there was something terrible and compelling about those eyes. He could not bear their scrutiny. He would have to blurt out the truth.

Ben opened his mouth. But before he could speak, Mr

Mallory said hastily, 'Oh, come now. That's going a bit far, isn't it? The boy's only been missing since last night.' He spoke the words 'last night' with a peculiar emphasis and looked hard at Ben. 'As you say, it's probably only a child's game. I shouldn't be surprised if he turned up sometime today.' He smiled. 'I hope, when he does, you won't be too hard on him. I wouldn't be.'

Ben looked at his father who continued to look back at him, his face suddenly gentle and smiling. His right eye – the eye farthest away from Uncle Joseph – closed in a barely perceptible wink. It was as if he was trying to tell Ben that he knew he had something to do with Thomas's disappearance but that he wasn't to worry, they would sort it out together, later on.

Ben's heart lifted, then immediately sank down again, into his shoes. Why should his father be on his side? Adults always stuck together. He was only trying to trap him into telling the truth about Thomas. Uncle Joseph had meant to trap him with that wily promise of a reward: his father was trying to trap him with gentleness and smiling. Perhaps it wasn't that, though. Ben did not really want to think his father could be so perfidious. Perhaps he was just miserable about how he had treated Ben the night before and wanted to say he was sorry ...

Ben said, in a flat voice, 'Can I go now, Dad?'

'If you want. But don't run away just yet. I'd like a little talk with you, later on.'

Again that wink – so small that it might have been a trick of the sunlight that was pouring into the room. Safely locked in the bathroom, Ben wondered about it. Was his father to be trusted after all? Ben thought and thought about it until his head began to ache and decided that he couldn't be sure. Grown-ups were unpredictable. They did too many things for your own good – and their idea of your good was never the same as yours – for them to be trusted absolutely. His father, though intelligent in many ways, was quite capable of deciding to give Thomas away, in order to keep Ben out of trouble.

No – the only thing he could be sure about now, was Uncle Joseph's wickedness. If he had needed anything to convince him it would have been that oily, 'dear little nephew' stuff and the stupid reasons he had given for not going to the police. Of course he didn't want to go to the police. He was a kidnapper – or he had intended to be. He would hardly go to the police and say, in effect, 'Will you find my nephew so that I can kidnap him, please?' It would be drawing too much attention to himself. Uncle Joseph wouldn't want that.

'My dear little nephew,' Ben said, in a mincing, disgusted voice.

In the living-room, Mr Mallory was saying, 'Well, I'm afraid I'm due at my office ...' He stood up. 'If there is anything I can do to help ...'

Uncle Joseph did not move from his chair. 'Your son was not telling us the truth,' he said softly.

Mr Mallory's mouth tightened. 'Indeed?' He decided that he liked Uncle Joseph less and less the more he saw of him.

But Uncle Joseph smiled pleasantly as if they were the best of friends. 'I have proof that your boy was in my house last night.'

'*Proof?* What proof?' There was an angry gleam in Mr Mallory's eye, which died when he saw what Uncle Joseph was holding out to him. He took Ben's penknife and examined the name and address carefully, as if it were still possible there might be some mistake. There was none.

'Yes, this is my son's,' he said. 'But – I don't understand how you knew he was here. This is his home address, in Henstable.'

'I looked up your surname in the telephone directory,' Uncle Joseph said simply. 'I knew the boy must be living locally, otherwise he could not have made friends with Thomas, could he? And Mallory is not a common name; when

I found that you were living only a few doors away from us, I guessed that this must be his home and that the address on the penknife must be an old one.' He paused reflectively before he added, 'But you said it was his *home* address. Does he not live with you?'

'No. He usually lives with his aunt, in Henstable. My – my wife died some years ago.'

'I am very sorry for that,' Uncle Joseph said in a hushed, sad voice. 'Is the boy fond of his aunt?'

'Yes. Very fond.' Though Mr Mallory felt, in an irritated way, that this was none of Uncle Joseph's business, he could hardly object to this questioning. It was quite clear that Ben had behaved badly to Uncle Joseph. He had broken into his house, persuaded his nephew to run away, and he had lied about it . . .

Mr Mallory sighed. He blamed himself, in a way. He should have suspected something before! There had been that astonishing interest Ben had showed in the affair of Chief Okapi. He should have known, then, that there was something odd going on: it was not like Ben to show interest in anything that did not immediately concern him. Instead, his suspicions had only dawned when Ben had made that plaintive little speech about having no friends in London; he had laid it on far too thick! And even then, Mr Mallory had only had the faintest of doubts. He had thought Ben was probably lying, why, he didn't know, but he had not wanted to accuse him in front of a stranger. As Ben had guessed, he was feeling ashamed about his anger of the night before. He should never have lost his temper with the boy like that. After all, it was *his* fault, really! He should never have gone out to the pictures with Shirley and left Ben alone . . .

Mr Mallory turned the penknife over and over in his hand, reproaching himself for many things, including one or two that were quite irrelevant, such as not taking Ben to a doctor about his adenoids. Finally, he lifted his head and looked at

Uncle Joseph. His face was without expression. 'Ben will be delighted to have this back,' he said.

Uncle Joseph smiled. His voice was gentle as a cat's purr. 'Perhaps you would like to give it to him now,' he said. 'In fact, *I* would like to give it back to him, since it was left in my house.'

Mr Mallory did not move.

Uncle Joseph said, 'Will you call him in, please?'

'Yes. Yes, of course I will.' Mr Mallory walked towards the door. Then he stopped. 'I hope you won't be too hard on him,' he said.

Uncle Joseph's smile broadened. 'Why should I be? I only want my nephew back,' he said.

II

'NOBODY WANTS US'

Bᴜᴛ of course, Ben had gone. It was too much of a risk to stay. He had no illusions about that 'little talk' with his father. He would be forced to reveal all he knew and that could only have one ending. Ben had to admit that Uncle Joseph had sounded quite horribly plausible, not like a kidnapper, but like an anxious uncle worried about his nephew. It would be useless to try to persuade his father otherwise.

He must warn Thomas. And then he must stay away from him. Even if his father had believed him when he told that lie, he knew Uncle Joseph had not. From now on, he would be watching Ben. Watching and waiting. Hoping that Ben would lead him to Thomas . . .

Suddenly Ben had a splendid idea. He could act as a decoy. He could pretend Thomas was hiding somewhere else, in any number of places. He could behave furtively; dodge down side alleys, catch buses to outlandish suburbs, run across the Park. He would glance back over his shoulder all the time in a suspicious manner. Uncle Joseph and his spies would be sure to follow him. Oh – what a dance he would lead them!

Ben's spirits lifted. By the time he reached Lil's garden he felt excited and immensely cheerful, so cheerful that he attempted Thomas's whistle. The trick was to dart your tongue backwards and forwards in your mouth . . .

He achieved quite a passable imitation of that marvellous, warbling note. Delighted, he pursed his lips for a further effort but Lil rose up from the undergrowth, her finger to her lips.

'What you making that awful row for?' she whispered.

'I was whistling,' Ben protested.

'Was *that* what it was?' she said in an affected, sarcastic voice, but before Ben had time to be offended, her manner changed. She grabbed hold of the front of his red jersey with both hands and said hoarsely, 'Oh, Ben, I'm glad you've come. I bin waiting and waiting. Something *awful's* happened.'

'Has someone come for Thomas?' Ben's heart missed a beat. Suppose Uncle Joseph's visit had been a trick to keep him out of the way while one of the others, Old Baldy, perhaps, tracked Thomas down . . .

But she shook her head. 'No. They come for *me*. The Welfare lady. She banged and hollered. Said she knew I was there an' if I didn't open up she'd get the key from the landlord. 'Course, I didn't say nothing. I jus' listened for a bit and then I took Joey so *she* wouldn't get him and we run out.' She paused, quivering all over with indignation. 'She said I'd got to let 'er in 'cause it was her job to look after me. Silly old cow.'

'Oh, I dunno,' Ben said awkwardly. Perhaps Lil really did need someone to look after her. She was so little and thin. Someone ought to feed her up and comb her hair.

But this was only a passing thought and he knew better than to mention it to Lil.

So all he said was, 'Where's Thomas then?'

'Down on the Site.'

'The Site?'

'Where all the kids play. I told 'im to wait for us.'

Ben was horrified. 'But that's not safe. I mean – he ought to be hiding.'

'It's safe as anywhere. You get all sorts of kids on the Site. No one 'ud think of looking for him there.'

The Site was a large, fenced-off area where they were demolishing two streets of old houses in order to build a new block of flats. There were no workmen there because there was a strike in the building trade.

'It was a bit of luck, really,' Lil said. 'S'not easy to find good places. My Mum says it was different when she was my age, just after the War. There were hundreds and hundreds of lovely bomb sites. She used to have a smashing time.'

'There's a good playground in the Park,' Ben said. 'With swings and a slide.'

'Swings,' Lil said scornfully. 'They're jus' for kids.'

Ben decided that he would never be able to find the site on his own. Lil was a Londoner, born and bred, and city children have their own routes, secret and devious as mouse runs through a street of old houses. She led him through a maze of alleys he had never known existed, across a railway line, through a shunting yard. They came out, finally, into a quiet street where there was a high fence covered with notices. No Admission. Trespassers Will Be Prosecuted.

Just below a large Danger sign, there was a loose board in the fence. Lil glanced up and down the street but it was empty except for an old dog sunning himself on the pavement. Lil pushed the loose board aside and wriggled through the opening like a fish. It was a tighter fit for Ben.

'Hurry up, fatso,' Lil said.

'I am *not* fat.' Red-faced, Ben squeezed his stomach in. A wrench and a tug and he was through.

It was a lovely place. No neighbouring building was high enough to overlook it. One side of the site had already been dug out and left a splendid open space in what had been the basements of old houses and shops. Now it was full of concrete mixers, piles of girders and empty oil drums. On the other side were the half-demolished houses with flights of stairs moving up into nothing-ness; torn-open rooms with wallpapers still clinging damply to the remaining walls and sometimes a fire-place, hanging dizzily in space.

'It's super,' Ben said, breathing hard. 'Supersonic. The best place I ever saw.'

Children swarmed everywhere, like mice. Big children, little children . . . Their voices were muffled by the high fence and the derelict houses.

'Why aren't they at school?' Ben said. 'I mean, school's started, hasn't it?'

'Only mugs go to school,' Lil said.

'Don't you?'

'I bin once, but I didn't like it. So Mum took me away.'

Ben was struck speechless. When he recovered his breath he said, 'But you have to. I mean, it's the law.'

Lil shrugged. 'You jus' have to watch out for the Truant Officer. He'll catch up on this lot sometime. Not me, though. It's all right if you keep on the move. Mum and me, we've always kep' on the move.'

Ben was filled with incredulous awe. Vistas of glorious, golden freedom opened up before him. 'D'you mean your Mum doesn't mind?'

'Mind? My Mum? She says she 'ad so much school when she was a kid, it turned her ignorant.' She looked at Ben. 'I bet I know more things than you do, though.'

Ben had an uncomfortable feeling this might be true. But he said stoutly, 'Bet you don't.'

'Bet I do.'

'What d'you know, then?'

She wrinkled up her nose and gazed at the sky. 'What's an Ai?'

'There's no such thing.'

'There is, then. It's a three-toed Sloth.' She wrapped her arms round her chest and hugged herself gleefully. 'What's an Anemometer?'

'*You* don't know.'

'I do then. It's an instrument for measuring the force of the wind.' She laughed at his flabbergasted face. 'I only know things beginning with A, though. Mum and me, we're working through the dictionary. We each learn some and then we have quizzes in the evenings. I'm jus' getting on to B.'

Ben could think of no comment to make on this original method of education. To conceal his envious admiration, he changed the subject.

'Where's Thomas?'

Lil led the way across the site to where Thomas was sitting on an upturned, old bath. Its rusty, claw feet stuck forlornly into the air. On his lap, he held the budgie's cage. Close beside him, two boys were fighting, quite amiably: their squeals and groans were for theatrical effect only. Thomas watched them.

'We've been practising wrestling holds,' he said to Ben. 'I got three submissions in the first round.'

This hardly seemed likely. The boys on the ground were filthy; the dust, which was everywhere, covered not only their clothes but their hair and faces with a uniform film of grey. They looked like coal miners just up from the pits. Thomas, on the other hand, looked as if he had recently dressed for a party. His white socks were not perfectly clean, perhaps, but they were still recognizably white. His silk shirt was tucked neatly into his trousers.

'You didn't,' Ben said.

'I did. Really, Ben . . .'

'You can't have,' Ben said. 'You can't have been fighting.'

Beside them, the larger of the two fighting boys was now sitting astride the smaller one and leaning on his spread-out arms. He looked up at Ben and Thomas. A grin of happy expectation appeared on his face which disappeared as the smaller boy jabbed him in the back with his knees, tipped him off, wriggled up and ran away. The bigger boy lingered a second before he dashed after him. 'Show 'im, Mate,' he said, to Thomas.

Thomas put down the bird-cage and stood up. He looked at Ben hesitantly.

'Come on,' Ben said. He advanced on Thomas, intending to try a hold he had seen at a wrestling match in the Public Baths. You thrust one leg between your opponent's and threw him backwards over your knee.

Instead, he found himself lying on the ground. Thomas was standing over him, smiling apologetically and holding out his hand to help him up. 'It was what Mr Baldry taught me the other day,' he said. 'Did I hurt you, Ben?'

Ben did not answer. He felt humiliated. He got up, brushing the dust from his clothes.

Lil said, to Thomas, 'You didn't oughter play silly tricks like that. You might've broke his back.'

Her feminine indignation restored Ben's good humour. 'Not with a proper Judo throw.'

She tossed her head. 'Well, I think fighting's plumb stupid.'

'It's just fun,' Thomas said. 'Girls do not understand.' He grinned companionably at Ben. 'Where are we going? Lil said you would think of a place for us to hide.'

'I don't know,' Ben said slowly. 'I haven't worked it out yet.'

Lil's eyes were bright and angry. 'I'm sure *I* don't know

how we're goin' to hide him,' she said. She looked at Thomas, scowling, and trying to think of some way she could get her own back. 'He looks so – so conspickus.'

'Conspicuous,' Ben corrected her with a certain amount of pleasure.

She glared. 'That's what I said.'

'I do *not* look conspicuous,' Thomas said passionately. He looked round the site. 'There are a lot of boys here who are dark-skinned, like me.'

Lil laughed contemptuously. 'S'not your skin, stupid. It's your silly clothes. I mean – jus' look at you. *White socks.* I mean, it ain't natural.'

Thomas looked hurt for a moment. He looked down at the offending socks, then, thoughtfully, at Ben. A slow smile spread over his face. 'I know,' he said eagerly. 'I know what to do. Ben must lend me some of his clothes. Then I will be disguised as a Peasant.'

Ben laughed. Thomas saw that he had said something funny and began to laugh too. He pretended to be ill with laughter and staggered about, clutching his stomach. Although Lil didn't understand why they were laughing, she became infected too. She giggled and stood on her hands, giggling, until the blood rushed to her head and made her giddy.

Then Ben realized it wasn't so funny after all. He couldn't go back to the flat and get clothes for Thomas. 'I can't do that because Uncle Joseph 'ud find out,' he said, and, when they didn't appear to take this in but went on with their giggling horse-play, he shouted frantically, 'Oh, do *listen*. Uncle oseph's been there, he *knows* about me. He's probably followed me now to – to track Thomas down.'

They both stood still and silent at once, though Lil was hiccuping a little.

'He can't – *hic* – have followed us,' she said, but she looked over her shoulder fearfully as if she expected Uncle Joseph to rise up suddenly among the cement mixers.

'Perhaps not,' Ben admitted. 'But he'll be on the look-out now. And – and if I once go back, then he'll set someone on to trailing me.'

He wondered if he should tell them his plan for being a decoy. He thought about it for a minute and then, reluctantly, abandoned it. He couldn't really leave Thomas. He was a stranger in England and though Lil was plucky and sensible, she was only young. And a girl.

Besides, he didn't really want to go home to the flat. It wasn't his home, anyway. And his father didn't really want him there, not just now. He wanted to get married to Miss Mackingtosh and take her away on their honeymoon: Ben's presence was just a nuisance to him. Thomas was a nuisance to *his* father, too. If Thomas wasn't in England, his father would be in no danger from him. They were, he and Thomas, both in the way; that was just about the size of it. He said gloomily, half to himself, 'No one really wants us, do they?'

Thomas was looking at him with a puzzled expression. 'What are we going to do, Ben?'

Ben thrust his hands deep into the pockets of his jeans. He felt Pin – his fingers fondled him lovingly – and then, farther down, something round and hard. He pulled out a two-shilling piece and immediately the world looked brighter. 'We're going to have some breakfast first,' he said. 'I'm too hungry to think.'

They found a coffee stall just outside the site. Ben bought them each a roll and cheese and Lil a cup of coffee for her hiccups. It came to one and tenpence altogether.

'Can I have another roll, Ben?' Thomas said.

Ben shook his head. 'That's all the money I've got. Just twopence left.' He frowned. 'We've got to have some money. I mean we can't just live on *air*.'

'Have you got anything to hock?' Lil said.

'What's that?' Thomas asked.

Lil sighed impatiently. 'Don't you know anything? You take something into a pawn shop and they keep it for you an' lend you money while they keep it. There's one down the road.'

'I could've hocked my watch,' Ben said. 'Only it's at the menders.' His watch was almost always at the menders.

'You can have mine.' Thomas stretched out his wrist and Lil and Ben looked at it in silence. Then they looked at each other. Gold watches were as conspicuous as white socks. 'It's got my name on the back,' Thomas said helpfully.

'That's a lotta good, ain't it?' Lil said. 'Why don't you just ring up your old Uncle Joseph an' say, here I am?'

'Oh, I wouldn't do that,' Thomas said, looking alarmed.

'Don't tease him, Lil,' Ben said quickly. 'Have you got anything?'

'Only Joey's bird-seed. I got one pound two an' fourpence in my post office book but that's at 'ome, under the mattress.'

Ben pretended to search in his pockets, though he knew all the time what was there. Pin. He took out the little jade horse and showed him to Lil. 'I've got this,' he said sadly.

'That's not worth nothing,' Lil said. 'Who'd give you anything for a silly old toy horse?'

Ben's eyes snapped. 'Like to bet me?' he said.

12

GOOD-BYE FOR EVER

THE pawn shop smelt musty, like an old cellar. There was a dim, fly-blown window full of old clocks and watches and, behind the counter, a long rail of old clothes.

An old, old man shuffled out of the dark regions at the back of the shop. He looked as if he dressed entirely in other people's clothes. He wore thick glasses on his enormous nose which was red and pitted like a strawberry.

He said, in a soft voice, 'What d'you want, sonny?'

Ben's fingers were curled tightly round Pin. He hated the idea of parting with him. But he had to – he had to. They had to have money. Even if he were willing to go without food for ever and ever, rather than sell Pin, he couldn't let Thomas starve.

He put Pin down on the glass-topped counter and said, 'I want to pawn my horse.'

When Miss Pin had given him the little horse he had said, 'I'll take care of him for ever.' He wondered what she would say if she knew what he was doing now. Then he thought that she would probably be excited by this whole adventure . . .

The old man picked up Pin. He fumbled slowly in his pockets and brought out a magnifying glass. While he examined Pin, Ben looked at his marvellous nose. It was like a clown's. Had he been born with it? Was it – could it be – false? He tore his eyes away, for politeness, as the old man sighed and put Pin back on the counter.

'Where d'you pick this up, sonny?' he asked in the same mild voice.

Ben swallowed hard. 'A friend of mine gave it to me for a keepsake.'

'A friend?'

'An old lady.'

'Hmm.' The old man regarded Ben thoughtfully. Ben looked him straight in the eye. He had read that this was a sign of an honest person.

It seemed to work. The old man said, 'What d'you want to pawn it for, sonny?'

Ben thought wildly. Why should a boy want money? Fireworks? No – November the Fifth was a long way off and you wouldn't pawn a valuable keepsake just for fireworks. 'I want to buy a present,' he said. 'For – for my auntie.'

'A present for your auntie,' the old man repeated. He sounded sceptical.

'It's her birthday,' Ben went on in a rush. 'And I want to get her something special because she's old and she's poor and she hasn't got any children of her own. And – and she lives by herself in an awful little room in a basement and I want to get her something to cheer her up.'

A lump came into his throat. How dreadful it would be if Auntie Mabel was really like that, old and poor and living in one small, horrid room. Superstitiously, he crossed his fingers.

The old man said, 'How much d'you want?'

'Five pounds,' Ben said.

'Eh? What did you say?' The old man cupped his hand behind his ear. His ears were large, like his nose; they were white and dimpled like a cauliflower.

'Five pounds,' Ben repeated.

'Five shillings. Well that seems quite reasonable ...'

'POUNDS,' Ben shouted. 'FIVE POUNDS.' He remembered what he had seen sometimes on tickets in shop windows. 'And it's Worth Double.'

'Too much,' the old man said.

He pushed Pin back across the counter but his eyes, Ben saw, were sly. Ben picked Pin up and put him in his pocket. 'All right, then,' he said, as if he didn't really care, and walked to the door. He was about to open it when the old man said, 'Wait a minute, sonny.'

Ben turned.

'Come here.' The old man crooked one knobbly finger and beckoned with a mysterious air.

Ben dawdled back to the counter, his hands in his pockets. The old man bent towards him and whispered, 'You're a good boy to think of your poor old auntie, like that. Not many boys would bother. I don't like to think of your auntie going without her birthday present.'

Ben kept his face blank. 'Oh, that's all right. She's used to having to go without things. She's had a hard life.'

'What were you going to buy her?' the old man asked.

Ben closed his eyes. Suppose Aunt Mabel was really poor and starving . . . He opened his eyes. 'A nice chicken and – and a bottle of port.'

The old man chuckled suddenly. 'Tell you what, I'll buy it off you. Privately. Twenty-five bob.'

Ben drew a deep breath. 'I'd rather pawn it. So I can get it back later.'

The old man watched him. 'I'm not allowed to deal with children. By law. A straight sell is different.'

'Oh,' Ben said. 'Oh.' He took Pin out of his pocket and looked at him.

The old man said cunningly, 'It would be a pity if your auntie went without her port.'

'Two pounds,' Ben said.

The old man looked pained. 'Do you want to ruin me? All right – as a special price, mind, and I'll lose on it – thirty bob. And that's my last word.'

Ben could see that it was. Anyway, he hadn't the heart to bargain. He nodded, without speaking. The old man shuffled over to his till, rang it up, and took out three ten-shilling notes. He pushed them across the counter. They were extremely greasy and crumpled.

A deep sadness came over Ben. He rubbed the little horse, very gently and lovingly, from the top of his fine, narrow head to the end of his flowing tail. 'Good-bye, Pin,' he said, and set him down on the counter. He looked at him, standing erect on his slender, beautiful legs and the lump rose in his throat, almost choking him.

'Good-bye for ever,' he murmured and left the shop without looking back.

13

THE TIMELY PANTECHNICON

Ben walked back to the building site, where Lil and Thomas were waiting for him. He walked slowly because he knew they would be expecting him to tell them what he had decided to do, and he hadn't thought of anything yet. He couldn't think of anything: his mind was too muzzy with grief over Pin . . .

He played wildly with the idea of running back to the shop and saying he had changed his mind, but, at once, he saw that would never do: Thomas was relying on him. But surely there must be some other way of raising money? If only he hadn't had Pin with him! Aunt Mabel had always said he shouldn't carry Pin around in his pocket. 'You'll lose him one day, mark my words,' she had said and tossed her head and sniffed in the way she had when she lost an argument but knew, all the same, that she was right.

Well, now she was right, though not in the way she had meant. She'd be able to say 'I told you so'. Ben sighed. He had a sudden longing for Aunt Mabel. If only she was here or he was safe at home with her, in Henstable, he would never complain about her again. She could say 'I told you so' and toss her head and sniff just as much as she liked . . .

It was at this moment that he saw the pantechnicon. He turned a corner and there it was, a large, green furniture van with these words painted on the sides: THOS. SMITH. FURNITURE REMOVALS. HENSTABLE.

The tailgate was open and three men in beige aprons were carrying the furniture out of a small house and putting it into the van. The van was almost full and very tightly packed. The men were now fitting in odd chairs, mattresses, an ironing board and a bicycle like the last, small pieces of a jigsaw puzzle.

Ben stood on the pavement and watched. It seemed a marvellous stroke of luck. Surely, somewhere in that van, there would be room for two small boys. Then he realized that although the van might have come from Henstable, it might be going anywhere . . .

A small, elderly man with a sad, pouchy face and a drooping moustache like an old walrus, set an armchair down on the pavement and mopped at his forehead.

Ben edged close and said in a casual, conversational voice, 'Hot work today.'

The man nodded. He looked tired and out of breath. 'Shan't be sorry to get finished, I must say.'

'I see you come from Henstable,' Ben said. 'Are you going back there?'

'After we've had our bit of dinner.' Suddenly, the man turned and looked at Ben suspiciously.

Ben said quickly, 'That's an awfully big chair. Can I give you a hand with it?'

The suspicious look on the man's face changed to one of surprise. The chair, in fact, was rather small. He regarded it for a minute and then grinned. 'You'd strain yourself. You have to get used to lifting.'

'It must be a very heavy job,' Ben said. An idea had come to him. If he made himself useful, the man might agree to give him and Thomas a free ride to Henstable. 'You don't look strong enough to be lifting heavy things,' he said cunningly.

'It's knack, not muscle,' the man said.

'You could show me. I'm a quick learner and I'm strong for my age. And – and you shouldn't be carrying this chair all by yourself. I mean you're much too *old*.'

'I'm not drawing my pension yet,' the man said shortly – and rather rudely, too. Then, holding the chair in front of him like a breast-plate, he marched up, into the van. When he came out again, he passed Ben without a glance.

Ben was very much annoyed. After all, he'd only been trying to help. He walked off, whistling loudly and ostentatiously to show the man he hadn't been upset by his abruptness. All right, then. If he wasn't allowed to earn a free trip to Henstable, he would take it. He had tried to be honest, but all he had got for his pains was rudeness. There was bound to be a moment when the van was unguarded, perhaps when the men were having their lunch. He and Thomas could hide among the armchairs and the mattresses, quiet and snug as mice . . .

Ben felt cheerful and excited. He began to run.

By the time he reached Thomas, who was waiting meekly by the loose board in the fence, his plan was fully formed. It all seemed so easy that he couldn't imagine why he had felt so uncertain and depressed. It might be tricky actually getting into the van, but once they got to Henstable, everything would be straightforward.

No one would think of looking for Thomas there. ('No one wants to go to Henstable any more, they want fancy continental holidays,' Aunt Mabel had said when she was grumbling about the vacant rooms in her boarding house.) They could hide in one of the beach huts. As it was the end of the summer holidays, the huts would be boarded up, but, as Ben had discovered long ago, boards are easily removed with a chisel and a sharp stone.

'We can collect cockles and things to eat and we can live in the hut,' he explained. 'They're quite big, there'll be plenty of room for two of us.'

'*What?*' Lil said in a high voice.

Ben looked at her. In the excitement of telling Thomas his plan, he had almost forgotten she was there. But she was there, of course, standing beside Thomas and holding Joey's cage in her hand.

'You wasn't thinking of leavin' me *behind*?' she said.

For a moment, Ben was too dumbfounded to answer. The

answer was, that he hadn't thought about her at all except as a useful person to hide Thomas while he was deciding where they should go. Now, he looked at her white, angry face and saw how stupid he had been. Of course she thought she was running away too. Otherwise she would never have brought Joey with her, and his packet of bird-seed. And equally 'of course', she couldn't come.

He explained gently. 'It 'ud be better if we were on our own, really. Two boys, running away and hiding is one thing. But two boys *and* a girl *and* a budgerigar – well it's just too *much*. Like a sort of organized *hike*. We'd be too conspicuous. Someone would be bound to notice us. And anyway, the Welfare people will be looking for you, won't they?'

'That's why I want to run away,' she said stubbornly. Her mouth tightened into a thin line.

'I know. But it's a silly reason,' Ben argued. 'I mean, they won't hurt you, or anything. Only look after you till your Mum comes back. It's not as if you were escaping from kid-nappers, like Thomas.'

'I want to run away,' she repeated. Her expression was ominous.

'Well, you can't,' Ben said crossly. 'Do be reasonable, Lil. Suppose we had to run, or something. How could we run, lugging that budgie . . .'

She put Joey's cage down on the ground. Her face had gone whiter still. Ben thought, with horror, that she was going to cry. But she didn't. She gave a little, choked gasp and flew at him like a small, angry cat, scratching his face and hitting him in the chest. Ben caught her wrists and held them. She wriggled and kicked; she was very strong for a girl.

'I hate you – I hate you,' she cried.

Then, suddenly, her mouth crumpled up and she sank into a limp heap on the ground. 'I wish I hadn't cleaned up your sore knee,' she sobbed. 'I wish I'd let you get poisoned and die.'

'Oh, Lil,' Thomas said. His brown eyes filled with tears as

if he were going to cry too. He looked at Ben sadly and reproachfully.

Ben felt sorry and embarrassed. He crouched beside Lil. 'Don't cry, please don't cry,' he said. 'I didn't mean to be horrible. But – you see – it may be dangerous. We can't take you on something that might be dangerous. Uncle Joseph might come after us.'

'I'm not frightened of a silly old Uncle,' she muttered.

'Well – it may be difficult and uncomfortable too. We might not be able to hide in the huts. Last year, the police kept a watch because people had complained about tramps sleeping there. If they're keeping watch now, we'll have to live rough – we might even have to sleep on the beach. It wouldn't be suitable for a girl.'

Her shoulders shook. 'I know what you think. You think I'll make a fuss. Well, I wouldn't, so there. I'd *like* to sleep on the beach an' – an' collect cockles and things. It 'ud be ever so romantic.' Her sobs grew louder. 'An' I can't stay here, it's jus' as bad for me. They'll catch me an' put me in an orphanage. My Mum was brung up in an orphanage . . .' She looked up. In spite of her weeping, her eyes were dry. They looked angry, not sad. She said vehemently, 'I'll kill myself if you leave me or – or I'll *tell* on you. I'll tell Uncle Joseph.'

'You wouldn't do anything so stinking mean,' Ben said, horrified.

'Of course she would not,' Thomas said suddenly. He was looking almost as angry as Lil. 'She is my good friend. She would not betray me. Please let her come, Ben.' He drew himself up. 'I will be responsible for her, I promise.'

They both looked at Ben as if he were their enemy. It was very unfair, he thought. Just because he was the eldest and had to make unpopular decisions. But he couldn't go back on what he had said. It wouldn't be safe to take Lil.

'All right.' He shrugged his shoulders. 'Do what you like. Only if she's to come, you can leave me out. I'm not coming.'

'Not coming,' Thomas repeated in a dazed voice. 'But you *must*. We cannot go without you.'

This was very flattering. Ben might even have weakened if Lil had not said, at once, ' 'Course we can, you great goop, 'Oo does he think he is? Field-Marshal Montgomery? Oh – leave 'im to stew.' She looked at Ben and added in a mocking voice, 'Fancy yourself, doncher?' She climbed through the loose board into the street; Thomas passed Joey's cage over the top of the fence and she set it down beside her. She poked her head through the gap and said, 'C'm on, Tommy boy. Say good riddance to bad rubbish,' and stuck out her damp, pink tongue at Ben.

Then she bent to reassure Joey who had begun to flutter unhappily against his bars, and the board swung back into place.

Thomas lingered. 'Are you really not coming, Ben?'

'No. But I'm not stopping you. If you'd rather go with her, that's O.K. by me. Two's company, three's none.'

Thomas said gravely, 'It is not that I would rather go with her. But she is in trouble, too.'

Ben stared at the sky.

Thomas looked hesitantly at the fence and said, 'I'd better go.'

'Who's stopping you?'

Thomas pushed the loose board aside. He went through the gap easily; he was almost as thin as Lil. He gave one last, sad look at Ben and was gone.

Ben stood still, his eyes burning. It was terribly unfair, after all he had done for Thomas: getting into trouble with his father, telling lies, selling Pin . . . One good thing was that he could go and buy Pin back now and afterwards he could go home and behave as if nothing at all had happened. He would have to stick to that lie he had told his father about Thomas. That might be difficult, but if he could manage it, nothing could happen to him and everything would be as it was before.

But 'before' had been very lonely and dull. Slowly, it began to dawn on him that he couldn't, decently, let them go off without him. Lil might be plucky and smart, but she was only young. And they had no money at all.

He forced himself through the fence. They were walking slowly up the road. He watched them for a moment, struggling with his pride. Then he called, 'Wait – wait for me.'

They turned, and he darted up to them.

He said, frowning sternly, 'I better come. You don't even know where the furniture van is. You'd get into an awful mess.'

Thomas's face brightened. 'Oh, Ben, I'm so glad,' he said.

Lil said nothing. She just looked sullenly up at Ben through her lashes which were long and silky and fair. Ben felt suddenly bursting with generosity. He said, 'I'm sorry I was cross. Of course you can come. I expect you'll be quite useful, really.'

14

'WHERE WAS YOU BROUGHT UP?'

Lil started being useful at once.

When they reached the furniture van, the old man in the beige apron was sitting on the dropped tailgate, eating a sandwich. The children passed him, pretending to be absorbed in the game of jumping over cracked paving stones. He took no notice of them and they stopped in the shadow of the van.

'The others must have left him on guard . . .' Ben whispered.

'S'easy to get rid of just one,' Lil said.

'How?'

'Ask no questions an' you'll hear no lies,' Lil said smartly.

'Jus' you hide till I tell you. An' take Joey, he'll get in my way.'

She seemed so sure of herself that the boys did not question her. They went into the front garden of the empty house and crouched behind the hedge. Squinting through the privet, Ben could see Lil wandering up the road, peering in the gutter. She stooped and stood up with something in her hand. Then she disappeared.

Nothing happened for a bit. The street was sleepy and quiet as Sunday. Ben yawned and the bones of his face gave a little *crack* that sounded alarming in the stillness.

But it was as nothing to the noise that came the next minute: a great, cracking, splintering sound from the front of the van. The old man leapt up from the tailgate like a Jack-in-the-box and rushed round the side of the van. To Ben's horror Lil was there, barring his way. Had she gone mad?

She caught at his arm and said in a shrill voice, 'Some boys broke your window, mister.'

The old man brushed her off like a tiresome fly. He vanished round the front of the van and reappeared, his face twisted with rage.

'S'awful mess, ain't it?' Lil said innocently.

He barely looked at her. Of course, Ben thought, she looked too small and young to do any damage. 'Where'd they go?' he demanded.

'They run down the alley. You c'n catch 'em, if you want. It don't go through, there's nothin' but a high wall an' a few dustbins.'

The old man muttered and ran off. Lil gave him a few seconds start, then waved at the boys. 'Quick. S'only a short alley.'

They jumped over the tailgate and into the van. Lil went first. 'We gotta get to the front,' she said.

Luckily there was a mattress standing on its side between a tall wardrobe and a chest of drawers. It was a spring mattress with plenty of give in it – enough, anyway, to allow Lil and Thomas through easily. It was harder for Ben; he had to push and prod – it was almost as if the mattress was a live thing, resisting him. But he managed at last, pushing Joey's cage in front of him, and the mattress plumped out again, behind him. He found himself, squashed against Thomas in a tiny space at the front of the van. It smelt musty from the sacking the men had used to cover the furniture and a little light filtered through from the small window that looked into the cab where the driver sat. Thomas and Ben peered through and saw the shattered glass, lying like hail on the seat.

Thomas said in a shocked voice. 'You ought not to have broken the window, Lil. It is against the law.'

'Oh, don't be a soft nut,' Lil said. 'And don't stand there, they'll see your heads. Thomas better get up here wiv me.'

'Here' was a small space under a table that had been perched on a chest of drawers and strapped against the side of the van. Lil crouched small at one end and Thomas sat at the other, dangling his legs.

'You'll have to work your feet or you'll get pins and needles,' Ben whispered.

Obediently, Thomas jerked his legs and the chest creaked.

'Go easy,' Lil said. 'This chest ain't strong.' She looked round in the gloom. 'Rotten lot of furniture they've got. Awful, gimcrack stuff.'

Ben thought this was rather impolite as they were, in a way, guests of the people that owned the furniture, but he didn't like to say so. After all, it was Lil's initiative that had brought them here. He would never have dreamed of breaking that window, not because he was afraid, but because he was naturally law-abiding. But then he would never have dreamed of not going to school or of going to bed in his clothes. Nor did he have Lil's marvellous contempt for authority. In fact, beside Lil, he thought gloomily, he was horribly respectable and priggish. To think he had despised her as a girl, to think he had tried to stop her coming! He felt ashamed and humbled. He said, in a gruff voice, 'You were jolly clever, Lil.' He hated apologizing, but sometimes it had to be done. 'I'm sorry I said all the things I did.'

She looked at him shyly as if she were not sure whether he were teasing her or not. Then she smiled. 'That's all right then.' She held out her hand with the little finger crooked. Ben linked his little finger with hers and they shook their hands up and down. 'Make friends, make friends, never, never break friends,' Lil said, and then added accusingly, 'You haven't said it.'

Ben privately thought the rhyme silly. Linking fingers was something he hadn't done since he was small, but she looked so solemn that he gave in and repeated the words quickly.

She gave a contented sigh. 'Now we're sworn for ever and ever.'

'Let me do it too,' Thomas pleaded but Lil's eyes widened and she put her finger to her lips. 'Hush up now,' she said.

Their hearts stood still and their bodies too. There were loud voices outside the van. They heard the clang as the tailgate was fastened up and someone opened the door into the driver's cab. Peeping through the small window, Ben saw a man bend over the seat and sweep off the broken glass. He was swearing loudly. Then he climbed into the cab. The back of his thick, red neck was only a few inches away from Ben's nose, on the other side of the glass. Another man got into the cab and sat in the passenger's seat. Ben sat on his haunches, his knees squashed on either side of Joey's cage. The bird began to twitter and cheep. Lil's peaky face leaned forward. 'Cover 'im up,' she whispered.

Ben tugged the red sweater over his head – a difficult operation in that cramped space – and slipped it over the cage. At the same moment, the engine started up with a shuddering roar. The floor of the van juddered. Ben was wedged so tightly that he had no difficulty in keeping steady but Thomas and Lil lurched forward. They were only saved from hurtling on top of Ben by Thomas's quick action. With one hand he caught hold of a spare strap that was flapping loose against the side of the van; with the other, he seized Lil's jersey. As the van swung round the narrow streets he managed to fasten the loose strap around Lil and himself so that they were pinned against the side of the van, like the furniture.

'You'd better get comfortable,' Ben said. 'We've got a long drive.'

It was a long drive; so long, that lulled by the noise of the engine and the shuddering of the van, they even fell asleep. It wasn't comfortable sleep. Their eyelids became intolerably heavy, the noisy, jogging world receded and then, a minute later, their heads would drop forward or their legs and arms would begin to prickle and they would be jerked awake again. As Ben had forecast, Thomas's legs went to sleep. They felt like leaden weights, dangling over the side of the chest. In the end, he jammed his feet up high, against a big wardrobe on the other side of the van. All Ben remembered from the first part of the journey was that whenever he came round from his uneasy doze, Thomas's legs were jerking and quivering just above his head.

After hours and hours it seemed, the van stopped. The men got out of the cab. The doors banged. Slowly and painfully, Ben heaved himself up from his crouching position and stretched up to look through the small window. He could see other lorries. 'It's a café,' he reported. 'I expect they've stopped for a snack.'

As he said the word 'snack' he became conscious of a hollow pain in his stomach. He said, 'I bet they're having baked beans or something.' He thought about baked beans – lovely, Heinz baked beans, coated with luscious juice. It brought the saliva into his mouth. '*And* they've had their lunch. Lot of greedy-guts.' He thought about other food he liked: mashed potatoes with butter, crisp bacon, curling at the edges, fried bread, roast chicken. 'I'll die of starvation,' he groaned.

'It has been proved that people can go without food for three weeks,' Thomas told him. He sounded as if he didn't altogether believe this.

'They must have special stomachs, like camels. I haven't. Mine's like a drum.'

'Stop moaning about your inside,' Lil said.

Just then the cab door opened – they can't have been eating baked beans after all, they had been much too quick – and Ben signed to Lil to keep quiet.

The men got in. The van started up. The children dozed. They woke, cramped and hungry, moved their stiff limbs and dozed again. It was hot as an oven and stuffy. They began to feel stupid and heavy; even during the moments of wakefulness, their eyes were not properly open. From time to time they made small, creaky sounds like sleepy birds. It began to seem that they had been in the van for ever and ever. There was no reason why the journey should ever end ...

But it did. They were all asleep when the van finally stopped. It was the crash of the tailgate falling on to the road that woke them. They blinked at each other, at first barely conscious, then with growing horror.

'What are we goin' to do?' hissed Lil, who was the most wide-awake of the three.

Ben did not answer. There was no answer. They could only wait. He sat with the sharp edges of Joey's cage cutting into his knees while a great deal of energetic banging and crashing went on at the end of the van. 'Careful – easy does it,' a man shouted, and the floor of the van lifted and swayed as something heavy was carried out of it.

Ben moistened his lips which were cracked and dry. 'We shall just have to run for it,' he said. He stood up, on his stiff, trembling legs, and began to help Thomas unfasten the strap that had secured him and Lil.

'I can't. My legs are shaky,' Lil said. Her voice was shaky too; her pale little face was more scared than Ben had ever seen it. Her fear made him gather his courage. He whispered in her ear, 'It'll be all right. We'll take them by surprise. I – I'll hold them off while you and Thomas run for it.'

He sounded confident but he didn't feel it. They were really outlaws now. They had broken a window and stolen a ride – no one was likely to be gentle with them. Lil and Thomas eased themselves off the chest of drawers and all three stood, cramped together, waiting. There was nothing else they could do.

So they waited while, piece by piece, the furniture was removed from the end of the van. Each minute discovery was coming closer and closer. Suddenly, the mattress in front of them sagged a little: one of the men had removed a supporting piece of furniture.

Lil's damp hand edged into Ben's. He held it tight.

'Cover your faces,' he whispered. 'Then they won't know who you are.'

His heart swelled with fear and pride. He had decided what to do. He would rush out first and dive for the nearest man's legs. Of course he would be caught, but if he was lucky, he could keep them occupied while the others escaped. If he was lucky...

And luck, after all, was on their side.

A man shouted, 'Like a cuppa, mate?'

'Whazzat?' *This* voice was so close, just on the other side of the concealing mattress, that they trembled.

'I said, the lady says would you like a cuppa, mate?'

There was a pause. They held their breaths. 'Oh, might as well,' the man said.

His feet made a ringing, iron sound on the tailgate. There was more talking outside the van. Then silence.

'*Now*,' Ben said.

He pushed the sagging mattress aside and stepped into the almost empty end of the van. The others followed.

For a moment they stood, blinking and stretching, in the evening sunlight. They were in a back street in Henstable; Ben recognized the small general store on the corner. The street was empty except for a very old man with a stick who was walking carefully along the pavement towards them. As he approached the van, he looked at the children. Although he was not really interested in them – there was nothing very surprising, after all, about three children standing by a furniture van – their guilty consciences smote them.

'*Run*,' Ben said, and they ran as well as they could, their poor, stiff legs wobbling under them. Ben held Joey's cage with one hand and Lil's wrist with the other. Thomas stumbled behind them, arrows of pain darting through the muscles of his calves. They glanced backwards over their shoulders apprehensively but no one observed them except the old man who watched them with faint surprise on his crinkled face. At the corner a terrier dog rushed out of the general store and snapped at their heels: it seemed to give wings to their feet.

They ran on, panting and gasping. Past the Fire Station, past the Ford garage, past the gloomy frontage of the King's Hotel. When they reached the church at the end of his own street Ben realized that, unconsciously, he had been leading them home, to the house where he lived with Aunt Mabel. 'We can stop a bit in the churchyard,' he panted, dragging Lil in through the narrow gate into that quiet, restful place where the grass grew long among the old graves and the yew trees creaked overhead. It was a good place to stop and get their second wind: they fell, grateful and exhausted into the damp, long grass and lay there while their pulses slowed down.

Ben whispered, 'My house is down this street – over there.'

Cautiously, they crawled close to the railings of the churchyard. 'That's where I live,' Ben said.

Aunt Mabel's house was called *The Haven* and looked, Ben thought, just like one. It was a tall, narrow house squashed between two other tall houses. It was an ugly house but the windows were warmly red with the evening sun and inside, Ben thought, with a sudden surge of homesickness, Aunt Mabel was probably making a cup of tea. She was always making tea. When, just at that moment, she came out of the front door with her shopping basket, it was all he could do to stop himself rushing out of the churchyard and hurtling himself into her arms.

Instead he whispered, 'Hide,' and they flung themselves down behind a large tombstone on which the faint, old carving was still decipherable: *Herbert Gentle, Master Mariner*.

Aunt Mabel was carrying a shopping basket and wearing an old felt hat pulled hard down over her straggly grey hair. She was talking to herself. 'Five lamb chops and Miss Pin's fish,' Ben heard her mutter. She passed within a yard of the children, on the other side of the railings. They peered round the tombstone to watch her walk down the street, turning her feet out ten to two as she always did.

'That's my aunt,' Ben whispered when she was out of earshot.

'She looks nice,' Thomas said.

'She is.' Ben gulped. 'She's the nicest person in the world,' he said fervently.

'Where's she going?'

'Shopping. She'll be going to get Miss Pin's fish.' He thought, with an ache in his heart, that this was his job when he was home. Miss Pin liked plaice for supper or, sometimes, a nice piece of haddock, fresh out of the sea. He said, 'We've got to go shopping too, if we're not going to starve to death.'

In the shelter of Herbert Gentle's tombstone, they made their plans. Lil must do the shopping. Ben would be recognized and Thomas, being black, would attract more attention than Lil. But first they would go down to the beach and find a place where Ben and Thomas could wait for her, out of sight.

Ben led the way, down back streets. The others followed

him, Thomas happily, Lil most fearfully. Unlike Thomas, she had not a trusting nature, nor had she travelled much: any town outside London was a strange country to her, bristling with danger.

After ten minutes' steady walking, they turned a corner and felt a breeze on their hot faces, a good, sea breeze, flavoured with salt and seaweed. Ben breathed deeply and appreciatively: this was better than London. He quickened his steps.

'What's that?' Thomas said suddenly.

'What's what?' Ben stopped and looked at his puzzled face with surprise.

'That – that *noise*.'

Nervously, Ben listened. But all he could hear was the sea, hissing on the pebbles with a sound like someone sweeping broken glass.

'It's just the sea,' he said with relief. 'Haven't you heard the sea before?'

Thomas shook his head. 'I haven't seen it either.'

Lil looked at him with scorn. 'Haven't seen the *sea*? Where was you brought up?'

'Africa, you nit,' Thomas said.

15

THE CAVE IN THE CLIFF

THEY came down to the sea on a deserted stretch of beach a long way from the pier and the Clock Tower, where a curve in the chalk cliffs hid them from the promenade. Visitors almost never came here, Ben knew; they preferred to stay by their parked cars on the front, near to the candy floss stalls and the shops and the fun fair.

'You just follow the cliffs round and you'll come to the town,' Ben told Lil. 'Are you sure you'll be able to find us again?'

She nodded, looking grim. If she felt nervous about her errand, she was determined not to show it. 'Jus' you look after Joey for me,' was all she said.

Ben gave her ten shillings. 'Get stuff that'll fill us up. Once the tide's right out we can collect cockles, but we want something now, for supper and breakfast. Bread and bacon and something to drink.' He looked at her sternly. 'No sweets, we can't afford to waste money on sweets.'

'Can't we have an ice lolly?' she begged. 'Jus' one each. Three fourpenny ones.'

Ben relented. 'All right. And matches. We want matches.'

She said, with a wistful look, 'Couldn't we have sixpenny ones? I'd like an orange lolly.'

In spite of his resolve, Ben felt his mouth water. 'Get a lemon one for me. Only buy them last, or they'll melt.'

'Do you think I'm nutty?' she said, and walked off, tossing her head.

Ben watched her until she was out of sight, then he ran to join Thomas.

Thomas had taken off his shoes and socks and was tentatively dipping his toes into the creamy foam at the water's edge. He splashed with his hand and then put his fingers to his lips. There was a surprised expression on his face.

'Can you swim?' Ben asked.

'I learned in the pool at home,' Thomas said, 'but this tastes different.'

Ben laughed. It suddenly seemed enormously comic that Thomas shouldn't know the sea was salt. Laughing, he stripped off his clothes and ran into the waves. The beach shelved rapidly; when the water came up to his chest he dived head-first to the bottom to pick up a handful of stones and shot back to the surface, leaping up out of the water like a porpoise. He shook the wet, limp hair out of his eyes and saw Thomas had taken off his clothes and was standing in white vest and pants, shivering.

'Come on, the sea won't bite you,' Ben shouted.

Thomas waded cautiously in, picking his long legs up high, like a stork. His eyes were screwed up. Ben splashed water into his face with the palm of his hand. Thomas flinched and then splashed back. Ben approached him, averting his face to avoid the flying spray and they came to grips with each other, fighting and struggling until the current tipped their legs from under them and they went down in a tangle of limbs into the cold, buffeting sea. They came up, blowing and spluttering. Thomas was gasping for breath but he was laughing too. 'It's super,' he said. 'Oh, it's super.' And he dived under the water to catch Ben's ankles.

Ben twisted away and swam out to sea. Thomas caught him up easily and they swam side by side, rolling on to their backs from time to time and spouting water from their mouths. After the first chill, the water became velvety warm; it was the air that struck cold now, not the sea.

As they swam, all the heat and exhaustion of the journey seemed to wash off them. When they got back to shore, they felt full of energy and chased each other up and down, stumbling and limping on the pebbles, until they were dry enough to put on their clothes.

They settled in the shelter of a breakwater with Joey's cage wedged into the shingle beside them, and skimmed stones. When they were bored with that, they set up an old tin and threw pebbles into it, until the tin became full and tipped over. They felt too idle to pick it up again and just sat there, leaning against the breakwater and watching a small boat with a red sail slip slowly along the horizon.

'After supper the tide will be right out and we can collect cockles,' Ben said drowsily. 'And we can light a fire and sit by it.'

He yawned, feeling wonderfully content. It was like the most perfect of holidays, he thought. They could do what they liked, when they liked. There was no one to order them about, no one to fuss. They could just lie here and sleep in the sun.

But Thomas was restless. Playing on a beach was new for him. 'Let's build the fire,' he suggested.

They collected driftwood; dry, light stuff twisted by the sea into fantastic shapes, and built a fire in the mouth of a small cave in the chalk cliffs. Then Ben realized that they had wandered some way from the spot where Lil had left them. He went to look for her and found her scrambling over a breakwater with her purchases: a bulging carrier bag in one hand and three ice lollies, held carefully aloft, in the other. She looked hot and cross.

'I've had such a time,' she said. 'The shops were all shutting and I had to *run*.'

She had bought two sliced loaves, bacon, three bananas, a bottle of lemonade, matches and a tin of tomato soup.

'That's all I could get. Bacon's pricey and the carrier was sixpence,' she said. 'I got the bananas cheap 'cause they're a bit too ripe.'

Ben looked at the tomato soup. 'We haven't got a tin-opener.'

'I thought you had a penknife with an opener on it.'

'I lost it,' Ben said, with a pang.

They went to the cave. Thomas had been exploring. 'It goes in a long way,' he said. 'It's super.'

They followed him in, sucking their ice lollies. The opening was small, but once inside, the cave hollowed out. Pale walls met high over their heads; there was a smell of chalk, wet sand and seaweed. 'There's a sort of funnel at the back,' Thomas said.

There was an opening in the roof. It led up and up, like a chimney, the white walls glimmering lighter the higher it went. 'I wonder where it comes out,' Ben said. 'It can't go through to the top of the cliff or I'd have noticed it. Perhaps it comes out half-way. I wonder if I could climb up and see.'

'You'd break your neck,' Lil said shortly. She wasn't interested in the chimney but looked round the cave with pleasure. 'I think this is jus' lovely. We could make a sort of house here. There's a little ledge we could use for a table an' we could make chairs out of sand . . .'

The boys ignored her. They were still staring up the chimney. 'If I stood on your shoulders,' Ben said, 'and sort of wedged myself into it, I could get up with my back against one side and my feet against the other.'

'Your legs wouldn't reach. They're too short,' Lil said, but Ben was already balancing himself on Thomas's shoulders and reaching for the mouth of the chimney. Once he was over the small lip of the opening, Lil turned out to be right.

'I bet Old Baldy could get up there,' Thomas said. 'I bet even I could. I'm taller than you.'

'Not that much taller,' Ben said crossly, dropping back on to the floor of the cave.

'I think I am.'

'You are not.'

'Oh, give over do,' Lil said, scowling at them both. When they took no notice, she stopped scowling and said, very sweetly, 'Aren't you hungry? I am – I'm fair famished.'

Ben looked at her. It struck him that she looked very pretty when she smiled in that coaxing fashion. He felt in his pocket for the matches she had bought. 'We'd better get the fire started, then,' he said.

They lit the fire which burned beautifully, the way driftwood does on a dry day, and soon had a fine, red heart of hot ash. How to cook the bacon was the difficulty: spearing it on sticks, which they tried first, was no good because the wood caught fire before the bacon had begun to cook. Lil went beach-combing and found an old skewer but that was no better: the metal quickly became too hot to hold and Ben dropped it, bacon and all, into the fire. Then Thomas produced a flat stone about twelve inches across. They laid it gently on the hot ash and rashers of bacon on top of it. The bacon twisted and curled, frying quickly in its own fat. The tips of their fingers burned as they fished it out but that was a small matter compared with the pleasure of that lovely, hot bacon, eaten between slices of soft bread. They had the bananas for pudding, washed down with lemonade drunk from the bottle, and then more bread, fried on the stone. They each thought privately that this was the least satisfactory part of the feast as the bread was salty and charred, but they ate it all, every crumb, and said, aloud, that they had never tasted anything better.

'Mm, that was *good*,' Lil said. 'No washing up, either.' She settled back comfortably against the cliff. 'Are we going to stay here? The beach huts ain't any good. I had a look when I went along the front. People are still using them.'

'I expect it's the fine weather,' Ben said. The news didn't dismay him much. It was so comfortable here and he was feeling lazy.

'Can we sleep in the cave, then?' Thomas said eagerly.

Ben stretched himself and yawned. It would be pleasant not to move, pleasant not to have to worry and make plans. 'Don't see why not,' he murmured, and yawned again.

Infected, Lil and Thomas yawned too. The sun was still warm and they were sleepy after their food. They lay on the pebbles, by the dying fire, and sank into a comfortable doze.

When Ben woke, the fire had died and the sun had gone, though the horizon was still streaked with red and gold and the rest of the sky was a clear, delicate blue, like a duck's egg. It was much, much colder. The tide had gone out leaving a broad expanse of shiny purplish mud.

He got up and went into the cave. Though a little light still filtered down the chimney, it was rather dark and dismal now. And the sandy floor was damp. A chill settled over his body and his spirits too. He hugged his arms across his chest and came out of the cave.

The others were stirring. Thomas said sleepily, 'Are we going to collect cockles, Ben? You said we could, after supper.' He didn't sound very enthusiastic.

Ben had no stomach for cockling either. 'It'll be dark too soon,' he said.

Thomas shivered.

'He's cold,' Lil said to Ben. She spoke accusingly, as if this was Ben's fault.

'I am not cold,' Thomas said. He stood up and stamped his feet and slapped his arms about valiantly, but he continued to shiver. His teeth chattered. 'I will go inside the cave,' he said.

Ben looked after him gloomily. 'It's colder in there,' he shouted, but Thomas didn't answer.

Lil said, 'He'll catch pneumonia. He's used to it being hot in Africa.'

'He can have my jersey,' Ben said bravely.

'I'm cold as well.' Lil opened the door of Joey's cage. The bird fluttered against the bars as she filled his dish with birdseed. 'I haven't got any water for him,' she said reproachfully, as if this was Ben's fault, too.

Ben waved a hand at the sea. 'Water, water everywhere and not a drop to drink.'

He had meant to make her laugh but she stuck her nose in the air. 'Think you're funny, don't you?'

'No,' Ben said, resigned. 'Is there any lemonade left? He can have that.'

She shook her head. 'Nuthing 'cept a bit of bread. Nuthing for breakfast. We're going to be awful hungry as well as cold.' She poked at the ashes of the fire with a stick. 'Fire's gone out, too.'

'Well, it was *you* wanted to come,' Ben said, goaded. 'You said you wouldn't complain, you said it 'ud be nice to sleep on the beach. *Romantic*, that's what you said . . .'

In spite of his sarcasm he was angrier with himself than with Lil. He ought to have planned better, he ought never to have let them go off to sleep, he ought to have known it would get cold like this once the sun went down . . .

'I didn't know it 'ud be so cold, I didn't,' Lil muttered. To Ben's horror, two fat tears coursed slowly down her cheeks. She rubbed at her eyes with her knuckles.

'Don't cry, Lil,' Ben said awkwardly. 'I'll fix something. Get some blankets or –'

He was interrupted by a shout from above.

'Ben, look at *me*.'

Astonished, they looked up. Lil forgot her tears. Thomas's face had appeared, grinning, apparently suspended half-way up the cliff.

'How d'you get up there?' Ben shouted.

'Up the chimney. My legs were long enough. I told you . . .'

They rushed into the cave. Standing underneath the chimney, they looked at its smooth, white sides with awe.

'I'm going to have a try,' Ben said, but Lil caught his arm.

'Don't leave me, Ben. I'm scared to stay by meself.' She looked over her shoulder and moved nervously closer to him. 'It's sort of dark an' ghostly . . .'

'Don't be silly. It's just getting dark, that's all.'

All the same, he made no move towards the chimney but shouted up, 'What's it like, up there?'

In answer, Thomas appeared at the top of the chimney. At least, they assumed he did – all they could actually see was that the light that came from the top was suddenly blacked out. They heard scuffling and scraping and then, peering upwards with straining eyes, could just make out Thomas as he worked his way down, looking like an agile chimney-sweep or a long-legged crab. He dropped on to the floor of the cave, covered in white chalk dust. 'It is not too hard,' he said. 'The first bit is the worst. After that it flattens out a little and there are handholds and little ledges. At the top there is another cave, thinner than this one with smaller caves leading off. There is one sort of passage that looks as if it goes a long way but I could see nothing. It was too dark.'

It was getting darker minute by minute. Ben looked longingly at the chimney but knew he had no time to attempt it now: if he was going to do what he had been planning to do, all the time Thomas was talking, he must set about it before the moon got up.

He said, 'I'll climb up tomorrow. There's no time now. I've got to do something. You both wait here for me.'

Lil's face was the palest glimmer in the darkness. 'Where you going, Ben?' she asked in a queer voice.

He said easily, 'To get food and blankets and a tin-opener.'

She gave a little gasp. 'I know what you're going to do – you're goin' home to your auntie . . .'

'Well – yes,' Ben admitted. 'But I won't be long. You wait here and I'll be back.'

'I bet you won't,' Lil said in a hollow voice. 'You won't come back, you'll jus' stay home. An' you'll leave *us* here, all by ourselves . . .' Her voice rose, she was midway between temper and tears. 'Softy,' she jeered. '*Softy*. Running 'ome to his Auntie Mabel. Poor baby, does it want its auntie, diddums den . . .'

'Be quiet, Lil,' Thomas said. 'Ben wouldn't leave us . . .'

'Oh – wouldn't he? That's all you know.'

'Of course I wouldn't leave you.' Ben was trying hard to keep his temper because he knew that she was, really, very frightened. He said patiently, 'While I'm gone, you and Thomas can light a fire – inside the cave, so no one'll see.'

That would get them warm, he thought and, more important, it would keep them busy . . .

Thomas said quickly and coaxingly, 'That would be fun, wouldn't it, Lil?'

Lil was almost convinced, but not quite. 'He might not

mean to stay home,' she said cagily, 'but he'll 'ave to, once he gets there, won't 'e? You don't think 'is auntie's jus' going to let him go 'ome and then come straight out again with all them blankets and things . . .'

Ben laughed. 'You didn't think I was going to ask her, did you? I'm going burgling . . .'

16

BEN GOES BURGLING

A few minutes later, Ben was away from the shelter of the cliffs and heading towards the town. A little, cold wind blew off the sea and flapped the deckchairs on the deserted promenade. As it was the end of the season, the fairy lights on the front were dead; only a few still sparkled along the length of the pier like a string of diamonds laid on the dark sea. The moon was not yet up and Ben flew, a darker shadow in the darkness, along small streets and side alleys until he came to the back wall of his aunt's house.

The gate into the back garden creaked as he slipped inside. There were lights at the back of the house; one in Mary's room, one in John's, and, on the ground floor a crack glimmered through Miss Pin's dark velvet curtains. Ben barely gave these windows a glance. He made straight for the coal chute into the cellar. It was covered with a concrete slab. It was the work of a moment to ease this gently off the top of the chute; his fear was that he had grown since he had last used this entrance and would be too big, now, to wriggle down the chute. But his luck was in. Aunt Mabel had not yet ordered her winter coal and, though the chute was a tighter squeeze than it used to be, he landed, a second later, on the floor of the cellar. He had

scraped the skin from his knee and blood had begun to trickle
from his old scar, but he was safe inside.

The cellar was black as pitch. He waited a minute or so to
gather breath, then, cautiously, he began to grope his way to
the small bench where John kept his scouting equipment. John
was an extremely tidy boy and although Ben had used to scoff
at him for his neatness, he saw now that there could be certain
advantages in it. He knew exactly where everything would be
and he was not disappointed: John's torch was hanging on the
nail where it always hung and Ben's searching fingers closed
upon it gratefully. By its thin beam he saw other things he
needed: John's duffle bag, packed with his sleeping-bag and
spare blanket, his tin-opener, his scouting knife, his cooking
pans . . . Ben felt them through the canvas and sighed with
relief. The duffle bag was narrow enough to go easily up the
chute and there was plenty of room in the top for a few other
useful things. He swung the beam of the torch along the bench.
There was a coil of fine, nylon rope John used for rock climbing. The water carrier was missing but there was the bottle
with the sprinkler top John used for watering the brim of his
scout hat to make it stiff. This bottle was half full of water.
Ben stuffed the nylon rope into the top of the duffle bag and
the water bottle into his pocket. He put the duffle bag ready on
the dusty pile of coal at the base of the chute, disturbing a few
stray lumps of coal which rattled down to the cellar floor. The
noise made him tremble; he stood in the darkness and listened.

There was silence.

He stood still, nerving himself for the more difficult part of
his venture. Then he tiptoed round the 'ell' of the cellar and
made for the short flight of wooden stairs that led up to the
kitchen. At the foot of the steps he stopped. The door at the
top was slightly ajar, letting in a crack of light from the kitchen.
Was Aunt Mabel there? She was careful of electricity and
seldom left lights burning in empty rooms. But, though he
strained his ears, he could only hear the faint hissing of the

old-fashioned boiler and the ticking of the alarm clock that Aunt Mabel always kept half an hour fast in an attempt to encourage the children to be on time for school. They had often pointed out to her that since they knew it was half an hour fast, it could hardly achieve this purpose.

Ben crept slowly up the wooden stairs, quaking each time they creaked. But there was still no human sound from the kitchen. He gained confidence. His hand was on the door, his muscles nerved to push it cautiously open when, suddenly, Aunt Mabel spoke.

'But if what you say is true, I can't think why my brother-in-law has not telephoned me.'

Ben froze, still as stone.

'Perhaps he didn't want to worry you,' a man's voice said. 'I understand that he didn't take the matter very seriously.'

'I expect he's right, then. He knows Ben. He's a sensible boy. And if they only disappeared this morning ...'

Who was she talking to? And where was she? Not in the kitchen, their voices weren't close enough. Ben pressed gently against the door and it yielded silently. He kept back in the shadows, ready to bolt if necessary. The kitchen was empty as he had thought, but the door into the hall was half open. Aunt Mabel was standing with her back to the opening, her hair gleaming and whiskery under the hall light. The remains of her supper was on the kitchen table: she must have just left it to answer the door.

Her visitor said, 'I'm afraid it is serious, though. I know young Thomas, you see. Your nephew may be sensible, as you say, but Thomas is headstrong and wilful. A bad boy. I'm afraid he may be a bad influence – get *your* boy into trouble.'

Ben almost laughed. Who could imagine Thomas being a bad influence on anyone?

Aunt Mabel did laugh, a queer sound, like a snort. 'No one could influence Ben. For bad *or* for good. *I* should know.'

She snorted again. 'You might as well try to influence the wind. Or a brick wall! Not that he isn't a nice, dear boy. But he's independent minded. Though there's nothing wrong with that, within reason.' She sounded thoughtful, as if she were having an argument with herself. 'Sometimes I think we hem children in too much. They need a bit of freedom – need to kick up their heels and stretch their legs occasionally.'

Ben felt indignant. Who hemmed him in, then, if it wasn't Aunt Mabel with her endless, 'wash your hands', 'have you done your homework', 'I'll thank you to keep your dirty boots off my clean carpet'?

The visitor said, 'I'm glad you can take it so lightly.' He spoke with a faint undertone of menace.

Aunt Mabel's voice changed. 'Oh – I *don't*. If I really thought any harm had come to my Ben . . .' She stopped and added, with sudden suspicion, 'I don't see, though, what made you come to me. Did my brother-in-law give you my address?' She paused and then went on with a tinge of irony, 'After all, you said that he didn't want to worry me . . .'

'The boy left his penknife behind when they bolted,' her visitor said flatly. 'We thought he might have brought Thomas home here.'

'Well, he hasn't. I haven't seen hair nor hide of Ben. I can promise you he's not here.'

Ben put his hand over his mouth to stop himself giggling out loud.

The visitor said, 'That's that, then. It was just a chance. We didn't want to leave any stone unturned. I suppose there's nothing for it now but to go straight to the police. Thomas has been missing since last night, so you can see we're very worried.'

'I can see that,' Aunt Mabel said slowly. Then, 'Oh, dear, I suppose it *is* serious, then. Perhaps you should go to the police. I don't know.' Her voice had become quavery and flustered. 'Perhaps if you would wait a minute, Mr – Er – I could telephone my brother-in-law. If you would like to wait in the dining-room . . .'

Mr Who? It wasn't Uncle Joseph, he was sure of that. Ben's curiosity was stronger than his fear. He drew a deep breath and darted silently across the kitchen to hide behind the half-open door. Through the hinge, he could see a flowered strip – a piece of Aunt Mabel's apron.

'In here,' Aunt Mabel said, and moved away. Frantically, Ben pressed his eye against the hinge. A strip of dark suiting came into his narrow line of vision, topped by a segment of gleaming, bald head.

Old Baldy.

Ben stood like a statue. He felt his spine prickle.

The dining-room door opened and closed. Presumably Aunt Mabel did not want him to hear what she said on the telephone. Alone in the hall, she stood still for a minute and said, 'Oh, dear, oh, dear,' in such an anxious, unhappy way, that it was all Ben could do to stop himself rushing out to comfort her. Then he heard her steps going to the telephone and the little click as she began to dial.

He would have liked to stay and hear what she said, but there was no time. She would be occupied for five minutes, at least. Long enough. Ben tiptoed, holding his breath, into the larder. There was a good piece of boiled ham on the marble slab, a packet of digestive biscuits and the remains of a chocolate cake. That was all he could safely carry as he discovered when he added a carton of eggs and dropped them on the stone floor of the larder.

Aunt Mabel hadn't heard – her voice was still talking on the telephone – but his courage broke with the eggs and he fled down the steps into the cellar. He stuffed the food into the top of the duffle bag, manhandled it up the chute and was out after it in a moment, stealing like a thief through the dark garden. No sound pursued him, but his heart thumped like an engine. He had not dared to stop to put back the cover of the chute, even though he knew it would betray him. She would know he had been there, she had so often scolded him for sliding down the chute and dirtying his clothes. And of course, she would tell Old Baldy . . .

Well, there was no help for it. They would just have to be extra smart, that was all. And why shouldn't they be? He knew the coast and the surrounding country like the back of his hand. There were hundreds of places they could hide, not only on the shore, but on the islands in the estuary and in the woods inland. As long as they were clever and sensible, they could stay free as birds . . .

In some mysterious way, the fact that he knew Old Baldy had tracked them down and that their situation was now perilous and difficult, lightened his heart. The treacherous pangs of homesickness that he had begun to feel disappeared altogether, now the hunt was on, battle joined . . .

He humped the heavy duffle bag on his shoulders and hummed a marching song under his breath.

'I left, left, left my wife and six fat babies, *right*, right, right in the middle of the kitchen floor I *left*, left my wife and six fat babies . . .'

He strode back to the cave like a hero.

Thomas and Lil greeted him like one. As they tumbled out his loot on to the damp floor of the cave, in the flicker of the driftwood fire, they were unstinting in their admiration. How clever Ben was, and how brave, to persist in his burglary once he had discovered Old Baldy's presence in the house!

'I'd never have dared. I'd have been scared to *death*,' Lil said, with a shiver.

'He might have caught you,' Thomas whispered.

'It wasn't anything, really,' Ben said modestly, but he sat back against the wall of the cave, proud as a pasha, and basked in their praise. In return, he praised them for the beautiful fire they had made and the enormous pile of spare driftwood they had gathered.

'We nearly got copped, though,' Lil said with a nervous giggle.

But it wasn't as dramatic as that. An old lady, walking her dog on the shore, had stopped and asked them what they were doing, out so late.

' 'Course, I jus' said to mind her own business, an' we run off,' Lil said. 'But she stood, peerin' after us. Interferin' ole cow.'

'I don't think she saw us very well, though,' Thomas said. 'She wore very thick spectacles. I think she was almost blind.'

'It doesn't matter anyway,' Ben said airily. 'We'll be moving on tomorrow.'

'Where to, Ben?'

'Wait and see.'

Ben realized that since he was now the acknowledged leader of the expedition, he couldn't admit that he didn't know. A leader, to maintain his position, must keep his doubts to himself, even if he has to be a little mysterious from time to time. His other job is to see that his followers are warm and fed and to keep their spirits up.

He gave Joey the water out of John's hat bottle. Then he sliced the ham with the scouting knife and all three made a satisfactory second supper. Clutching a piece of chocolate cake, Lil settled down in the sleeping-bag and Thomas and Ben shared the blanket. Thomas's feet were cold and Ben gave him his red sweater to wrap round them.

The fire sank to glowing embers. They were warm and comfortable.

Lil said drowsily, 'I wonder how my Mum is. It's sort of funny, thinking of her in hospital.'

'My mother is in America,' Thomas said.

Lil sighed. Thomas stirred restlessly. Ben saw that they were both sad and a little homesick once more.

'Mine's dead,' he said, to cheer them up by reminding them how lucky they were, but it had the opposite effect.

'Oh – poor Ben,' Thomas said with a catch in his voice and Lil turned her head to look at him. There were tears in her eyes that glinted in the firelight.

'She died a long time ago,' Ben said. 'Too long ago to be sad. Aunt Mabel's more like my mother, really.'

This was true, but Lil and Thomas thought he was just being brave about it. Their admiration for him increased. Thomas felt for Ben's hand under the blanket and gave it a little squeeze.

Lil said, 'You've got your Dad though, haven't you?'

She choked on a little sob. Ben lifted himself on one elbow and looked at her. She was lying on her back, staring upwards.

'Haven't you?' She was silent. He said gently, 'When's your Dad coming home, Lil?'

'I dunno.'

'What d'you mean?'

'What I said. *I dunno.* Why don't you wash your ears out?' She paused and then went on in a rush, 'He han't bin home for a twelve month. Mum don't know where 'e is. He jus' went off, after Old Baldy . . .' She gave a little wail and buried her head in the sleeping-bag.

'Go on?' Ben said, interested. 'What did Old Baldy do?'

The sleeping-bag wriggled. Lil's head poked out again. She gave a deep, deep sigh. 'I dunno. Least – I do know, a bit. 'E lent my Dad some money, last time he was home. Dad lost his pay on the dogs, see, an' he was skint. So he borrowed off Old Baldy. He didn't oughter have done it – Mum was hopping mad – but 'e did. Then he couldn't pay it back an' Old Baldy started comin' round and threatening him. I heard 'em shouting one night after I was in bed. Old Baldy was tellin' a lotta lies. He was trying to make out he 'adn't lent my Dad the money – that my Dad had just took it off 'im, one night when they was in the pub. An' my Dad said it wasn't true, he'd jus' borrowed it, an' Old Baldy said he'd had enough. 'E said 'e was goin' to the police. Then he went 'ome and my

Mum and my Dad had an awful row. It was after that my Dad went off . . .'

'But haven't you heard from him since?' Ben said, astonished. 'Haven't you had a letter?'

'Not a flippin' post card, even. My Mum don't know where 'e is an' Old Baldy don't know neither. He keeps stopping me in the street. "When's your Daddy comin' home, Lily dear?" he says, ever so soft and sarky. An' he does the same to my Mum. "Any word of your 'usband, Mrs Bates?"' Her voice trembled with passion. 'I jus' *hate* Old Baldy. Him an' his horrible money! My Mum's paying it back, five shillings a week. She takes it across to him Friday nights, regular.'

Thomas said, 'I think he must be a very mean man. To take five shillings a week from your mother.'

'Stinking mean,' Ben agreed.

But Lil said surprisingly, 'No, *that* ain't mean. What's mean is all that sarcastic stuff an' threatening my Dad wiv the police. But it's right to pay the money back. Dad borrowed it. My Mum says she won't rest easy till it's paid off. She's very straight, my Mum.' She was silent for a moment and then she said in a queer, strained voice, 'My Dad's straight, too. He jus' scares easy, that's all. I don't tell my Mum 'cause it upsets her but I think he's jus' stayin' away till he's saved up enough to pay Old Baldy back. Then he'll come 'ome and tell Old Baldy where he gets off!' Her voice rose triumphantly.

The boys said nothing, and after a minute she went on in a quieter, more doubtful voice, 'Do you think that's it, Ben?'

'I expect so.' Ben felt, suddenly, rather sad, but he could feel her eyes looking at him: they seemed to be pleading for something. He did his best. 'Perhaps he's gone on an extra long and difficult voyage to make more money,' he said. 'Danger money. That's what you get on – on expeditions to the South Pole and things like that. Or – or perhaps he's been shipwrecked somewhere on a desert island. Somewhere where the coastline's dangerous and ships have been wrecked before.

He might even find an old shipwreck – a Spanish galleon or something. Loaded with bullion. Then when he comes home he'll be able to pay Old Baldy off ten million times – he'll be a millionaire.'

Lil laughed. 'That's jus' a fairy story for kids.' But she sounded comforted. She gave a little, happy sigh and snuggled down in her sleeping-bag.

No one spoke. The fire made a soft, whispering sound. Ben began to think of the difference between borrowing and stealing. It was sometimes very difficult to draw the line. What had he done this evening? Breaking into your own house and taking your brother's scouting equipment was only borrowing. But the boiled ham and the cake and the biscuits – *that* was stealing. Even if Aunt Mabel would forgive him – she wouldn't want him to go hungry, after all – there must be no more of it. From now on, they must be straight, like Lil's Mum. They would have to live on what they could catch. They could get cockles and mussels, perhaps even crabs at low tide if they went up to the big sewer that ran out into the sea beyond the pier. And there would be nuts in the wood, and blackberries. He knew where there was an especially good patch, growing in a cutting by the side of the railway line . . .

Thomas gave a little snore and turned over, pulling most of the blanket with him. Ben tugged back as much as he could and then turned himself so that he was back to back with Thomas and his side of the blanket was pinned firmly under his body.

He became aware that Lil was looking at him. The fire was almost dead now, but there was enough light to see the dark pools of her eyes.

She said, in a soft voice, 'I do love you, Ben. I shall love you for ever. Do you love me?'

Luckily, before he could answer this embarrassing question she gave a long yawn, closed her eyes and went to sleep.

17

TRAPPED

WHEN Ben woke, the moon was fully up. A weird, pale light whitened the walls of the cave. But it was not the moonlight that had wakened him. It was the hollow booming of the sea.

He sat up, wondering. There was another boom, like a roll of drums, and then the tinkling crash of slithering shingle. A sharp wind flew into the cave like an icy breath and the flaky ashes of the fire flurried up like snow. It was followed by a new sound, a long, rushing sigh as the first, spent wave trickled into the cave and sank into the sand beneath them.

'Wake up,' Ben shouted. Two startled faces, eerie in the moonlight, turned towards him. He leapt up and ran to the mouth of the cave.

What he saw, turned his bones to jelly. The wind was high, hurling the sea against the cliff. Ben stepped outside the cave. The wind slammed into his chest like a giant fist and a ridge of yellow foam curled up to meet him. The sea sucked round his knees. For a terrifying moment he thought he would be dragged down but he fought his way back, against the heavy pull of the current, and stumbled against Lil just inside the mouth of the cave.

'What's the matter?' she said, rubbing her eyes, still only half awake.

Ben didn't answer. He dived frantically for the torch and swung the beam round the cave. It showed him what he should have noticed before: the seaweed, clinging high up on the chalk walls. He stretched up to touch it. It was scabby and dry: the sea only reached here at a very high tide. But this was a high tide . . .

'We're caught.' His voice squeaked high with alarm. 'Caught by the tide.'

'What is a tide?' Thomas asked. He was not frightened, why should he be? He knew nothing about the sea.

But there was no time to give him a geography lesson. Ben said quickly, 'The sea's coming in. We've got to get out.'

'But we can't,' Lil wailed from the mouth of the cave. She was wide awake now. 'The sea's all round. We'll be drowned.'

'We can swim,' Thomas said. 'We had a lovely swim this afternoon.'

'I can't swim,' Lil cried. She darted to Ben and clung to him in terror.

He put his arm round her, partly to comfort her, partly to comfort himself. 'It wouldn't help if you could. No one could swim in *that*.'

Thomas investigated for himself. 'No, we could not.' His face was wet with spray. 'It is as if the water were boiling,' he said excitedly. 'Will it swallow up the cliffs, Ben?'

'Don't be a dope. Only in here – high up, where that weed is.' Ben forced himself to be calm. He lifted the torch again. 'There's a sort of shelf up there but it's too small. We'd slide off it.'

Lil began to cry. 'We can't get out,' she sobbed.

'We can climb up the chimney,' Thomas said.

They stared at him. '*You* can,' Lil said. 'What about us? Ben and me? Selfish pig.'

Ben said, 'Don't be mean, Lil. There's no point in us all drowning.' Then he remembered. 'You won't drown anyway, don't cry. There's the rope . . .'

Lil was light. Thomas could pull her up on the rope. But not me, he thought, *not me*. He thrust this thought away from him and dragged the coil out of the duffle bag. The floor of the cave was already awash and the things were sodden.

'Put the food in the duffle bag,' he ordered Thomas, while

he fastened the rope round Lil's waist. She stood passive, though she was shaking from head to foot. When the rope was knotted, she said wildly, 'Joey – I won't go without Joey.' Her tears burst out again.

'Thomas can pull up his cage,' Ben comforted her. 'And the duffle bag.'

'The ham is wet,' Thomas said regretfully.

'It'll dry out. Just shove it in. Fasten the other end of the rope round your wrist and climb up if you can.'

The next few minutes were so busy that he hadn't time to think of his own plight. He gave Thomas a leg up into the chimney and posted Lil on a dry rock beneath it. Then he stuffed the blanket into the mouth of the duffle bag and tied the thick draw-string in a loop to take the rope.

The noise of the sea filled the cave and the chimney and Thomas's voice floated down, light and thin as a bird's cry.

'It's quite light up here.'

Ben made a trumpet with his hands. 'Can you belay the rope?' If there was a jutting rock in the upper cave, it might take his weight, too.

But there wasn't. 'It's all smooth,' Thomas called. 'But if I wedge my feet against the side I can hold Lil . . .'

He only just managed it, though. The first part of the chimney was the difficult part: it was smooth and straight and Thomas had to take all her weight. There was a horrible moment when she felt the rope slacken and cried out. Thomas flung himself backwards, hauling on the rope with all his strength and jerked her higher, to where the chimney sloped forward and there were footholds in the crumbly chalk. From there onwards, Lil went up like a fly – though she was small, she was wiry and strong. From below, Ben heard Thomas's jubilant shout. Then, after what seemed an interminable wait, the end of the rope snaked down towards him. He fastened it through the loop at the top of the duffle bag and through the hook on Joey's cage. He jerked on the rope and the duffle bag and the cage rose slowly up the chimney to the accompaniment of Joey's wild squawking.

Ben stood still. He felt very cold, his heart was like a lump of cold lead in his chest.

'Your turn,' Thomas shouted thinly. 'If we both hang on hard . . .'

Ben hesitated. The rope dangled invitingly before him. He reached out to touch it and then, with an effort, put both hands behind his back and locked them together. The risk was too great. He was too heavy. He would only drag them both down.

His voice came out in a hoarse croak. 'It wouldn't be safe.'

He didn't wait for their answer but stumbled into the middle of the cave, leaving temptation behind him. He stood there for a minute, the sea swirling round his feet. His feet felt numb, his brain felt numb. He looked up at the small ledge he had seen before. Even if he could get there, it would be precarious. Could he hang on, clinging like a piece of seaweed to the walls, while the sea sighed and pounded in the cave? Once the tide was fully high, there would be very little room up in the roof of the cave, there would be very little air . . . He gasped suddenly. Even now, the cave seemed terribly small. If he was going to die, he didn't want to die here, in this stifling, shut-in place. Was he going to die? Fear closed his throat until he felt as if he were choking. He gasped again and rushed outside the cave.

The wind hit him, the spray soaked his face, he was knee deep in water, but he could *breathe*. He lifted his face to the wind and drank it in, in deep, grateful gulps. He looked up at the cliff. High up, in the chalk, he could see the black hole which was the mouth of the upper cave but the cliff beneath it looked frighteningly sheer and slippery – polished, almost, in the white light of the moon. He could never climb it. If he tried, he would fall on the rocks and be killed. They would find him, dead, his body washed up by the tide. Or perhaps they would never find him. There was a sudden, hot feeling in his throat and tears pricked his eyes.

Then he saw the big wave. It was the biggest wave he had ever seen. Still some way out, it was travelling towards him steadily, the creaming lip curving over the black underbelly. It would reach him any minute – any second. It would sweep him off his feet, suck him down. For a moment he was paralysed with fear, then he twisted round and leapt blindly for the cliff, landing on a crumbling, chalk spur. He embraced it with arms and legs and, miraculously, remained there while the giant wave broke over him.

He pressed his face against the cold cliff. He was wet through and trembling but after a little he began to breathe more steadily. He must try to climb up. It was a frail chance, but it was the only chance he had. If he stayed where he was, the sea would dash him against the cliff. It would break him like an egg.

He edged his way slowly sideways and upwards. His feet and fingers found what the flat light of the moon had concealed: a foothold here, a handhold there. Up and up he went, spreadeagled against the cliff like a small, black crab. Once or twice he had to stop, too scared to move. Once he slipped and slithered heart-stoppingly downwards before his wildly clutching fingers caught at a jutting edge of rock. Once he thought he heard Thomas calling him but he was too spent to answer, too afraid, even, to look up and see if he was crawling near his goal.

When he had almost given up hope, he reached it. The cliff seemed to yawn open in front of his face, and there was the cave. 'Thomas,' he groaned. He crawled to safety on his knees and elbows and lay, exhausted, on his face.

Thomas's voice came from a long way away. 'Ben – Ben. Wake up.'

Then Lil. 'He's dead. Ben's dead,' she choked. He felt her

cold hands, stroking the hair back from his face. Then her cold, salt-wet lips pressed gently against his cheek.

Ben sat up. 'I'm not dead, stupid. I'm just wore out.'

'Oh, Ben,' she cried, and dived at him again. He let her kiss him once more, then gently pushed her away.

'Didn't you hear us? We shouted and shouted,' Thomas said. 'We had no idea what had happened to you.'

'Did you climb up the cliff?' Lil asked.

'D'you think I *flew*?' Ben was restored to health by this ludicrous question. 'What d'you think I am! A blooming *bird*?'

'I would never have dared,' Thomas said. He crawled to the edge and looked down into the abyss. Then he said, in a wondering voice, 'Look – oh, just look.'

Out as far as the horizon, the sea seemed to be boiling; in the white moonlight every foam-capped wave stood out with shadowless distinctness. Above the wild sea the moon rode in the wild sky, high and clear and still above the flying black rags of clouds. It was a marvellous, dramatic sight.

'Pity the poor sailors,' Lil said.

'I'm going to be a sailor when I grow up,' Thomas said. 'I like the sea. Is it like this every night?'

'No,' Ben said. 'Least, I've never seen it. We're awfully *lucky*.'

Though they were tired, soaked through and shivering, the others agreed with him. Who would want to be in a dry, warm bed when they could sit in a cave, watching the sea boil? They fell silent for a while. Then Lil said suddenly, 'Let's sing something. It'll get us warmed up.' She sang, in a high, fluting voice:

'There was a man called Michael Finigan,
　He grew whiskers on his chinigin,
　The wind blew them out an' the wind blew them in ag'in
　Poor old Michael Finigan, begin ag'in .. .

The second time round Ben joined in. The third time

Thomas had got it, and joined in too. Then they sang 'The bear went over the mountain', 'How much wood could a woodchuck chuck, if a woodchuck could chuck wood', and several versions of 'Sam, Sam, the dirty man'. Lil knew more songs – or more versions of the songs, anyway – than Ben did, and Thomas knew none at all, but he was a quick learner. The one he liked best was:

> 'I went to the pictures tomorrow
> I took a front seat at the back,
> I fell from the pit to the gallery
> And broke a front bone in my back.
> A lady she gave me some biscuits,
> I ate them and gave her them back.'

As they sang, they huddled together and watched the sea. Their ice-cold feet, their sodden clothes, ceased to matter; they sang while the storm blew itself out and the sea calmed. In spite of occasional yawning fits, they were still singing when the sky began to lighten. But by the time the sun came up like a ball of orange jelly, they were all fast asleep.

When they woke, the sun was shining in their faces. The tide was so far out that it was almost impossible to believe it had ever been buffeting at the cliffs beneath their cave. 'We can go cockling,' Ben said. 'We'll have cockles for breakfast.'

They couldn't climb down the cliff – when Ben looked to see the way he had come up the night before, it gave him an unpleasantly queasy sensation in his stomach – but they could climb *up*. The mouth of their cave was quite close to the cliff top and a tiny track, like a sheep or goat trail, led them there.

They ran on the green turf, whooping and shouting, to where the cliff was lower and easy to scramble down. Then they raced across the shingle to the shiny mud, squealing with laughter as they sank ankle deep into it. They giggled and shouted in an almost stupidly light-hearted way, as people do when they have been in terrible danger and come through alive. Once Thomas fell on his back and lay there, laughing, in the sticky, evil-smelling ooze.

When they had all sobered down a little, Ben taught them how to catch cockles. You watched for the sign – the tiniest of wrinkles in the smooth surface of the mud – then you dug down quickly with your fingers and seized the small, shelled creatures before they wriggled right away.

It was hot work. They steamed, as the sun and their exertions dried the clothes on their backs; by the time Ben judged they had collected enough cockles for a reasonable breakfast, they were completely warm and dry and every trace of stiffness had disappeared from their limbs.

The matches had remained fairly dry in Ben's pocket and, though it was a harder job than yesterday, they managed to get a fire going in the lower cave. They roasted the cockles on a stone, tied them in Thomas's handkerchief and toiled along the beach, up the cliff and back to the upper cave.

They ate the cockles with ham and damp, sliced bread. The ham had not suffered much from its wetting except that it was somewhat saltier than it had been, but the bread was rather nasty and the cockles were nastier still.

'We ought to have vinegar,' Ben said. 'Cockles are rotten without vinegar.'

'I'm awfully thirsty,' Lil said, pulling a face. 'All that salt. I never want to eat salt again.'

Ben looked at John's hat bottle. 'There's only enough water for Joey. Suck a pebble,' he suggested.

Lil tried, but spat it out at once. 'That's salt too. Ugh.'

'We'll get some water later,' Ben promised her. He yawned, he felt remarkably sleepy. 'When we've explored the cave and digested our meal.'

The cave was long and thin, no more than a narrow slit in the cliff that widened out to a small platform at the entrance. It narrowed as it went back, rising slightly and then falling, so that you did not see the top of the chimney until you were upon it. The hole took up the width of the cave at this point but, by climbing on to a ledge, it was possible to get beyond it. Here, the cave hollowed out; there were a few, smaller caves in the walls but they were no more than niches, just big enough for one person to curl up inside. At the very end there was a kind of passage, a dark hole that seemed to lead straight into the cliff. Ben crawled in but it was dark and queer-smelling so he was unwilling to go very far.

'I suppose we could hide in there if we had to,' he said. 'If anyone came after us, I mean.'

Thomas and Lil were stretched out in the mouth of the cave, relaxed in the sun. They looked sleepy as owls. Thomas yawned till the tears came. 'No one will come after us,' he said. 'We're quite safe here.'

18

'OH, BEN – MY POOR, DARLING BEN'

THEY slept the morning away. The long night had exhausted them and their sleep was sound. They did not stir when three people passed below them on the beach, searching carefully in every cave and inlet. Ben only woke when he heard Aunt Mabel's anguished cry . . .

Aunt Mabel had had a worrying night. Although Ben had heard her talking on the telephone, she had not, in fact, been talking to Mr Mallory but to the operator on the local telephone exchange. The high wind, that later on that night was to whip the sea to such frightening fury, had already swept across part of southern England leaving a trail of damage

behind it: falling trees, crashing chimney pots, broken telephone wires . . .

It was like a small hurricane, the operator told Aunt Mabel.
Most of the telephone lines to London were down and it was
unlikely they would be repaired that night. If she tried to ring
again in the morning, they would hope to be able to put her
through.

Aunt Mabel thanked the operator and put the telephone
down. She stood for a minute, thinking. She understood, now,
why Ben's father had not telephoned her: he had not been able
to. Poor man, how worried he must be!

Then a new thought struck her, one that made her heart
beat faster. Perhaps Mr Mallory had not been *trying* to telephone her! Perhaps Ben was not missing, after all! It was only
this bald gentleman, sitting in her dining-room, who had said
that he was. Why should she believe him? She had not much
liked the look of him – he had a shifty air – and he had not
even told her his name. If there really was an African boy
called Thomas, why should his uncle not come to look for him
himself? Suppose the bald man was an imposter – a thief who
had concocted this story in order to get into the house? Aunt
Mabel, who was a great reader of crime stories, knew that
thieves often sent a member of their gang to look over a house
before they burgled it in order to find out if there was anything worth stealing. Casing the joint, they called it. Suppose –
suppose he was even now counting her silver spoons or
examining the hall-mark on the beautiful cake stand that had
belonged to her mother!

Aunt Mabel's colour rose. She marched straight into the
kitchen and advanced on the ancient boiler. Though she did
not doubt her ability to deal with this bald-headed rogue
single-handed, it would be a sensible precaution to be armed.

She picked up the heavy poker that stood beside the boiler
and turned, the light of battle in her eyes. Her gaze swept the
kitchen and fell upon the open larder door. She went to close

it automatically – even a thief in the house could not interfere with Aunt Mabel's tidy habits – and she saw the mess Ben had left behind him on the larder floor. He had trodden in the broken eggs as he ran, and his slimy, yellow footprints led straight to the cellar.

Aunt Mabel gave a cry and dropped the poker ...

After that, of course, she doubted Old Baldy no more. Ben had certainly been here: his trail was plain to see. An ordinary thief might have stolen John's duffle bag, but he could not have wriggled down the coal chute, nor would he have stolen a half-finished chocolate cake.

'Ben is particularly fond of chocolate cake,' she said to Old Baldy who began to smile and then checked himself as he saw the unhappy look on Aunt Mabel's face.

She went straight to the police, taking Old Baldy with her. He was somewhat unwilling – it was no part of *his* plan to call in the police – but Aunt Mabel was adamant. And few people, as Ben could have told him, could hold out against Aunt Mabel once she was roused. 'Don't you want to find your Thomas?' she had asked, suspiciously, and Old Baldy, quailing before the expression in her eyes, gulped and nodded.

She was less successful with the police sergeant on night duty. He was sleepy and he also had a very bad cold which made him disinclined to take any action that was not absolutely necessary. To reassure Aunt Mabel, he took a light view of the matter. Boys went missing every day, he said, and, in his experience, they always turned up safe and sound. Besides, he added triumphantly, glad to find a good reason for doing nothing, *these* boys could not properly be called missing, could they, since she knew they were in the neighbourhood? They had food and blankets, a night out would do them no harm. They'd turn up in the morning, like bad pennies. If they didn't, it would be time to worry then

Aunt Mabel was not comforted. Old Baldy snored the night

away in a guest bedroom but she sat up in the kitchen, waiting and listening, the kettle on the stove ready to make hot drinks for the runaways as soon as they appeared.

At first, she had no doubt that they would soon tire of their adventure and turn up quite soon. It might have seemed a good bit of fun in the beginning, to camp out for a night and scare everyone to death, but it could hardly be fun now, in this terrible storm. It was a dirty night for young heads to be out in; from time to time, when the wind screamed extra loudly down the chimney or rattled the window in its frame, she went to the front door and looked hopefully up and down the bleak, empty street.

As the night wore on, however, hope died. Whatever Ben was up to, he was determined to go through with it. What *was* he up to? If it was just devilment, surely he would have given it up and come home by now? Had he run away in earnest, then? If he had, why had he done it? Was he unhappy? Why was he unhappy? What had she – or his father – done? 'Oh, my poor head aches,' Aunt Mabel said aloud, and fell to thinking of all the times she had been cross with Ben or unkind to him. (She had not often been unkind, only sometimes rather sharp-tongued which it was her nature to be, but her loneliness and despair made her think she had.) Towards the end of her long vigil, she cried a little.

With the first light, she woke Old Baldy. He was inclined to grumble, being averse to early rising, but Aunt Mabel's grim face deterred him. He got up, dressed, and accompanied her, meekly enough, to the police station.

The Superintendent saw them. He agreed that the boys' disappearance looked much more serious now, after the stormy night, and promised to send out a search party. They tried to telephone Mr Mallory again. The men had been working all night on the broken lines and this time the operator was able to get the number after a short delay. Mr Mallory's telephone rang but he did not answer it. While Aunt Mabel hung on, listening to the bell ringing and ringing in the empty flat, Old Baldy slipped out of the station on the pretext of buying cigarettes, made a telephone call of his own, from a public box, and had a conversation with Uncle Joseph in London.

When he returned, ostentatiously smoking, Aunt Mabel was getting into a car with a young policeman. Old Baldy joined them and Aunt Mabel explained that it had occurred to her that the boys might be hiding in one of the beach huts. Several winters ago, John and Ben had broken into one of the huts and camped out there for the best part of a day before a policeman discovered them and hauled them ignominiously home.

'I was angry with them,' Aunt Mabel said. 'Damaging other people's property! I sent them to bed without any supper. And it was only a bit of mischief, really – I don't know what made me so hard on them.'

Old Baldy didn't answer and Aunt Mabel blew her nose loudly. If they found Ben hiding in a beach hut, she wouldn't be hard on him now. She would never be hard on him again . . .

But the doors of the beach huts were padlocked as their owners had left them. There were no broken windows, no sign that a board or a shutter had been interfered with. 'They've not been here,' the policeman said. 'Maybe they're hiding in one of the shelters on the front. Tramps often do . . .'

But the shelters were empty. The beach was empty too except for an old, fat woman, walking her dog. As Aunt Mabel got back into the car, she came slowly and rather breathlessly up the steps to the promenade where she stood waiting for her old dog who was even fatter and more breathless than she. While she waited, she watched the police car curiously. There were a lot of old ladies like her in Henstable who had very little to do but walk their dogs and watch other people.

Aunt Mabel knew this. On an impulse, she wound down the window and called out, 'Can you help us? Have you seen two boys? We're looking for my nephew and a little African boy . . .'

'You're wasting your time,' Old Baldy muttered, but the old woman walked up to the car. Her eyes, behind thick spectacles, looked vague and anxious, but she was not as blind as Thomas had thought her.

'I saw a little black boy yesterday,' she said. 'Yesterday evening, down by the cliffs. I thought it was rather late for a child to be out. He was with a little girl . . .'

'A girl?' Aunt Mabel said, puzzled.

'An extremely *rude* little girl. I spoke to her – I thought it my duty as it was so late in the day – and she told me to mind my own business. They ran off to the cliffs, then. Really – she *was* rude. People bring their children up so badly nowadays, letting them roam about at all hours and be rude to people. I'm sure I don't know . . .'

She went on, complaining in her thin, reedy voice. She was a lonely old woman who had very few people to talk to.

Old Baldy said, under his breath, 'I told you you'd be wasting your time,' but Aunt Mabel got out of the car.

'How far?' she asked.

'About half a mile. It's –'

'A wild goose chase,' Old Baldy complained.

Aunt Mabel said, 'I don't mind how many wild geese I chase as long as I find my Ben.'

They tramped along the beach. The fine weather had broken at last and, although the sun was still warm, a cold wind blew in their faces and made their eyes water. The beach was empty and still but far out, almost at the horizon, a rippling, silver line showed that the tide had turned.

It was Aunt Mabel who found the lower cave. She glanced in, saw that it was empty and was about to turn away when her eye was caught by a streak of red. The sweater – Ben's red sweater – was half hidden by a mass of shingle that had been tumbled on top of it by the sea. Aunt Mabel pushed the shingle aside with her foot and bent to pick the sweater up. Beside it was another object, sodden and stained by the sea but still recognizable as John's sleeping-bag. For a moment, Aunt Mabel stared unbelievingly at both these things. Then a dreadful cry burst from her throat. She stumbled out of the cave and the policeman hurried up to her. 'He must have hidden here,' she said, her voice hoarse with horror. 'And the sea – that terrible storm . . .'

The policeman said gently, 'This belongs to your boy? Are you sure?'

He took the spoiled garment from her. It didn't look like a sweater any more, just a tangle of wet, red wool.

Aunt Mabel turned on him, eyes blazing. 'Do you think I don't know? I knitted it myself. Red's his favourite colour. He was so pleased with it. He would wear it all the time. I was cross with him for wearing a good new sweater to climb trees. I – I boxed his ears once when he tore the elbow out. Oh – to think of it . . .' Her voice trailed thinly away. She said gaspingly, 'If you don't believe me, his brother's sleeping-bag's still there in the cave.' Her pale face went paler still. 'Oh, Ben, oh, my Ben . . .'

She broke down and wept, her poor face buried in her hands. The policeman patted her helplessly on her heaving shoulders. 'Come on, now,' he said gently, 'I don't suppose it's as bad as that . . .'

There was not much conviction in his voice. He was a local man, he knew this coast and how the treacherous sea swept up, surging into the cliff. He glanced meaningfully at Old Baldy who was standing by the mouth of the cave with absolutely no expression on his face and said, sadly, 'I think we'd best get her home.'

Old Baldy nodded. 'I'll fetch the sleeping-bag,' he said. 'I daresay your superintendent will want to see it.'

He ducked inside the cave and looked sharply round him. He saw the tide-line of seaweed, high on the white walls, then he lowered his gaze to the ground and saw something else: the remains of a fire. He pushed the ashes aside with his foot, put his hand down on the flat stone and felt that it was still warm. He glanced round the cave thoughtfully and then he suddenly smiled, lifted his foot and kicked damp sand over the fire. When it was completely hidden he smiled again, as if at some private joke, and came out of the cave carrying what remained of John's sleeping-bag.

In answer to the policeman's inquiring glance, he shook his head. 'I'm afraid there's nothing else,' he said.

'Oh, Ben,' Aunt Mabel sobbed. 'My poor, darling Ben.'

Old Baldy looked at her. 'You're right,' he said to the policeman. 'Home's the best place. She could do with a nice cup of tea.' Then, for some curious reason, he raised his voice to a shout. 'There's no point in searching here any more. No point at all . . .'

The policeman was astonished. What was the man doing, trying to burst his ear drums? Then he remembered that when people were upset, they often behaved strangely.

'You mustn't give up hope, sir,' he murmured, and took Aunt Mabel's arm.

A flicker of a smile crossed Old Baldy's face. 'I won't. Not yet,' he said in a normal voice and stationed himself on Aunt Mabel's other side. The two men assisted her, very tenderly, back to the car.

Once she was comfortably seated in the back seat, white-faced but dry-eyed now, Old Baldy spoke rapidly to the policeman. Then, as the policeman got into the car and started the engine, he stepped back and raised his hand in solemn farewell.

He watched the car out of sight before he began to walk slowly along the front. He glanced at his watch, went into a café and ordered a raspberry sundae. When he had finished it, he sighed, and sat for a while irritably picking the pips out of his teeth. Then he looked at his watch again. He had a long time to wait for Uncle Joseph. He ordered a plain strawberry ice.

19

LIL IS IMPORTANT TOO

In their hiding-place, the children lay still as mice. For a long time, they did not dare move or speak.

Ben was torn by a mixture of emotions. He had not heard all Aunt Mabel said, her voice had been so choked with tears, but he had heard enough. Her grief brought a lump into his throat and tears into his eyes. He had known Aunt Mabel loved him, in the same unthinking way he had known the sun would rise every morning, but he had never thought that if he were to die she would cry like that . . . Nor had he ever thought that she might feel guilty about the times she had been cross with him, the way he sometimes felt guilty when he had been naughty or unkind. When he had heard her, sobbing over his old red sweater, it was all he could do to stop himself shouting out, 'It's all right, Aunt Mabel. I'm here,' partly because he longed to comfort her and partly because it would be such a gorgeously dramatic thing to do – to appear before her suddenly, as if he had risen from the dead.

Along with pity for Aunt Mabel went a quite different feeling, one he was slightly ashamed of: the feeling that it was, in a way, such a splendid *joke*. Here he was, alive and well, and soon John and Mary as well as Aunt Mabel, would be mourning his premature death. 'He was too young to die,' he could imagine them saying, 'poor Ben, poor, darling Ben.' How sorry they would be, how they would wish they had behaved better to him when he was alive, how they would cry . . .

Thinking about it, he wasn't sure whether to laugh or whether to cry himself.

He said, in a strangled whisper, 'They think we're dead. Drowned and dead.'

Lil giggled and then clasped her hand over her mouth as if afraid the walls had ears.

Thomas said, 'It's all right. No one can hear us.' He drew a long breath. 'Your poor aunt is very unhappy, Ben. I am sorry for that. But it means they will not look for us any more – it means that we are safe now.'

'No it don't,' Lil said.

They looked at her, surprised. She flushed up. 'Old Baldy don't think we're dead. Else why should 'e say what 'e did, about not looking for us any more? I mean ter say – why did he *shout it out*? As if Ben's auntie was stone deaf or something. I reckon he thought *we* might 'ear him.'

Ben frowned. 'But if he guessed we were here – I don't say he did, mind – but *if* he guessed, why didn't he just say so and make them go on looking?'

' 'Cause he didn't want to nab Thomas while the copper was there,' she said smartly. 'Stands to reason. If Old Baldy wants to kidnap Thomas – well, he wouldn't want the copper to know, would 'e? Kidnapping ain't legal.'

Ben looked at her admiringly. 'I didn't think of that. That's jolly clever, Lil.'

'Mum says I'm pretty sharp for my age,' she said comfortably.

Ben decided to ignore this. 'I expect I'd have thought of it in a minute. It was just Aunt Mabel being so upset. It took my mind off Old Baldy.'

'What are we going to do?' Thomas said. He sounded scared, but then, Ben thought, he had every reason to be scared. It was him Old Baldy was after . . .

'I don't know,' Ben said. 'Be quiet a minute, both of you. I've got to think.'

He stood up and walked slowly to the back of the cave, as far as the top of the chimney, his hands deep in his pockets. If Old Baldy had guessed they were still alive, then what would he do? What would *he* do, if he were Old Baldy? He would wait until he was free of Aunt Mabel and the policeman and then he would come back. Could he really have guessed where they were? How had he guessed? They hadn't made a sound . . .

Lil said, 'C'n I say something, Ben?'

Ben turned. 'If it's important.'

'P'raps Old Baldy saw our fire.'

'That's a good point, Lil,' Ben said, rather ashamed that he had not thought of this himself. 'But even if he did, he couldn't have known we were hiding up here, could he?'

It seemed to him that this was a good point, too. Clearly, if Old Baldy had seen the remains of the fire and guessed it was theirs, he might suspect they were still somewhere about. He couldn't know where. He could only shout on the off-chance that they would hear him and be lulled into a false sense of safety so that when he came back, in his own good time, he could catch them unprepared.

The trouble was, they couldn't be sure when he would come back . . .

Ben said slowly, 'I think the best thing we can do is to stay here. It's safe as anywhere. If he does come back to look, he'll never think of looking up here. Even if he noticed the chimney, he'd never think we could climb up it. He . . .'

'But I don't want to stay here,' Lil burst out. 'I'm thirsty. I want a drink.'

'Then want must be your master.' Ben quoted Aunt Mabel sturdily enough, though he was suddenly aware that his own mouth was cracked and dry. Lil wasn't the only one who was thirsty, he thought. Trust a girl to make a fuss about it! He ignored the ominous trembling of her lips and said crossly, 'You'll just have to put up with it. What we've got to do is to lie low and keep quiet so Old Baldy won't know we're here.'

Lil stared at him with horror. Suddenly, she let out a loud wail that echoed round the walls of the cave. 'I ca-an't. I'm thir-isty.'

'*Ssh.*' Both boys turned on her.

Thomas added, 'He may be outside now – waiting and listening.'

The thought of Old Baldy silenced Lil. She went white as a piece of paper. It silenced Ben and Thomas, too. All three sat, in silence, on the platform at the mouth of the cave.

They made themselves as comfortable as they could. But lying low and keeping quiet is one of the most difficult things in the world. Fear of Old Baldy helped them at first but, after a little, fear faded and the discomfort and boredom of their predicament crept into the forefront of their minds. They had no idea of the time, since Thomas's watch had stopped after the soaking it had received last night, and somehow this seemed to make the waiting worse. They were cold, too. The sky had clouded over, at first with the delicate, feathery clouds that are called mare's tails and, later, with thick cumulus like soft banks of grey, cotton wool. The wind had got up again and moaned against the cliffs and over the beach. It seemed impossible to believe that only this morning the sun had shone warmly and they had run and laughed and collected cockles ...

Thomas dozed a little. Lil fed Joey some bird-seed and played with him for a while, letting him perch on her finger and peck and flutter his long tail feathers. When he began to chatter and cheep, she put him back in his cage with the blanket over him to keep him quiet and then sat, staring out at the cold sky and the cold sea that was slowly creeping inland over the purple mud.

An hour passed, perhaps two. Ben thought, by his stomach, that it must be about lunch time when Lil said suddenly, 'Ben – Ben ...'

She was huddled up, her legs drawn up to her chin. 'I'm so thirsty I feel sick,' she said.

She looked sick. Her face had gone a queer yellow colour and there were dark hollows under her eyes.

'Try sucking another pebble,' Ben whispered.

She shook her head. 'I'd *be* sick. I want some water.'

Ben crawled over to sit beside her and coaxed her gently. 'You got to be brave, Lil.'

'I bin brave. I can't any more. Oh, Ben – is there any left of Joey's water?'

He tilted the bottle and shook his head. 'Not a drop. You gave him the last.'

She looked miserably out of the cave. 'I c'd drink the whole sea, every drop.'

'Salt water's no good. It would only make you worse. It might drive you mad – or kill you.'

'I 'spect I'll die anyway,' she said faintly, and Ben looked at her with concern. Could you die if you went without water just for one day? He pleaded with her. 'Just wait a bit longer, Lil. Just till it's dark. Then we'll go up on the cliffs and go down to the town and get water from the fountain in the park – all the water you want. Then we'll find somewhere else to hide.'

'I'm tired of hiding.' Her voice shook. 'I want to go home. I want my Mum,' she said and began to cry slowly and softly in such a weak, helpless way that the boys were appalled.

Thomas whispered, 'I think we should try to get her water, Ben. I'll go. I'll take the water bottle and . . .'

'You *can't*,' Ben interrupted him. 'He might catch you.'

This was just the sort of thing Old Baldy would be expecting them to do. Perhaps he was even now hiding at the foot of the cliff, waiting for hunger or thirst – or just boredom, maybe – to drive them from their hiding-place.

Thomas stood up. 'I'm going to get Lil some water,' he said calmly.

Ben looked at him. He said, in a low, stern voice, 'If Old Baldy catches you, he'll take you back to Uncle Joseph and Uncle Joseph'll take you back to Tiga. You don't want that, do you? I mean – that's why we've been hiding.'

Thomas's mouth set in a firm, proud line. He looked more

obstinate than Ben had ever seen him. 'I'm not afraid of Old Baldy,' he said.

Ben said frantically, 'You've *got* to be frightened of Old Baldy. Not for yourself, because you're not important. It's your country that's important. And your father. If you go back to Tiga that'll be the *end*. The end of your country and of your father, too. You've got to think of him and be frightened for him and you've got to *stay* frightened.'

He saw that Thomas was looking frightened now – and be-wildered, too. He said in a stifled voice, 'But that's what Uncle Tuku said . . .'

'I know,' Ben began, and stopped. *Of course*, he realized – he had never told Thomas how he had spied on them all that night. And there was no time to explain it now. He went on, quickly, 'What would your father say if he knew you were going to let him down just to get someone a drink of water?'

'My father?' Thomas looked at Ben. The fear faded from his face and he smiled. 'My father would say that Lil is im-portant too,' he said gently.

Ben looked at Lil. She was scrunched up small, her head fall-ing on to her chest. Her eyes were closed.

'We cannot let her die,' Thomas said.

'She won't die . . .' All the same, Ben saw that Thomas was right. Lil was just as important as Chief Okapi – more impor-tant, perhaps, because she was here and Thomas's father was a long way away. An idea came to him and he said suddenly, 'Where is your father, do you think? Will he have gone to America yet?' Because if he was safe, in America, they need not worry any more.

Thomas shook his head. 'He would not go to America without me.'

Ben thought. Then he said, 'I know what to do.' He felt so excited and triumphant that he almost laughed. 'I'll go. I'll go up the cliff way and get Lil some water and then – then I'll go to the police. Old Baldy's scared of the police. I'll tell them

Old Baldy's after you and ask them to find your father. I mean – it isn't as if Uncle Joseph was here . . .'

Thomas was staring at him stupidly. Ben sighed impatiently and went on, 'Don't you *understand*? Uncle Joseph's your uncle – the police would never believe *he* was a kidnapper. But Old Baldy – well, he couldn't pretend to be a *relation*, could he? Even if the police don't believe me, they wouldn't hand you over to Old Baldy, would they? They'd try and get hold of your father . . .'

Thomas said slowly, 'But suppose Old Baldy has really guessed where we are. Suppose he is not waiting on the beach, but up on the cliff? Suppose he catches you?'

'I can run. I can run jolly fast,' Ben boasted. Then he added, more realistically, 'Even if he does, I can fight and holler. And then, if you hear me shout, you can get down the chimney and run – run along the beach till you get to the town. Then you must go straight to the police station and – and give yourself up. You can ask anyone where the police station is.'

'What about Lil?' Thomas asked softly.

They looked at her. Ben said, 'She'll have to stay here. She can hide in the back of the cave till we come back. She'll be all right.'

Ben was less confident than he sounded. Would Lil agree? He crouched beside her and explained gently what they had planned to do, terrified that she would start to cry and say that she did not want to be left alone. But she was too sleepy and ill to protest; she only grumbled when they made her move and led her to the back of the cave. 'Is Thomas going too?' she murmured but she did not seem to listen to Ben's answer.

'Only if Old Baldy catches me,' he said. 'But you'll be quite safe. Someone'll come back, quite soon, and bring you some water – lots and lots of water.' He helped her up into the passage and put Joey's cage beside her. She moaned a little through her dry, cracked lips but then she settled down and seemed prepared to sleep.

Shortly afterwards, Ben left the cave.

Thomas crouched in the entrance, listening. After the crunch of Ben's footsteps had died away, he could hear nothing except the scream of gulls and the sighing of the wind. Ben must be almost to the top of the cliffs by now, he thought, and held his breath. Then he heard something new – a rattling sound as if someone had disturbed a shower of little stones. It came, not from the cave, but from below . . .

Thomas frowned. He was about to crawl cautiously to the edge and peer down the cliff, when he heard Ben cry out. It was a high, thin, frightened cry that rang out with startling suddenness for the space of perhaps two heartbeats, before it was cut off.

Thomas stood up. This was the signal he had been waiting for – and dreading: the signal for him to climb down the chimney and get away as fast as he could. But he moved one step towards the top of the chimney and then halted, every muscle taut and quivering. He couldn't – he couldn't run away and leave Ben in danger. He *was* in danger, Thomas knew – and it must be danger of a kind he had not expected. He had been prepared for Old Baldy – if he had been there, Ben would certainly have shouted a warning. But it would have been a shout, not that brief, panic-stricken cry. Perhaps Ben had slipped, perhaps he had fallen down the cliff . . .

The thought of Ben, lying stunned and helpless, drove all caution from Thomas's mind. He rushed out of the cave and darted up the cliff path. He did not stop to look down. He did not see Old Baldy climbing *up*.

Nor did Old Baldy see him. The climb absorbed all his attention: even for an athlete, it was a difficult feat. Ben had only managed it by miraculous good luck and because the darkness had mercifully hidden the terrible risks he was taking. Old Baldy could see these risks only too plainly. He crawled his way up, inch by painful inch, concentrating with every nerve and muscle and trying to make no noise. He intended to trap Thomas unawares.

As the boys had feared, he had been watching from the beach, though he had not been watching long. He had waited in the café most of the morning, staring gloomily out at the slowly clouding sky and eating ice-cream. By the time Uncle Joseph arrived, Old Baldy was feeling rather sick and liverish. He told Uncle Joseph about the fire in the lower cave, and led him straight to the shore. The two men searched the beach: if the children had not been dozing, they would have heard the crunch of their feet on the shingle. Old Baldy pointed out the upper cave, which was more visible from the beach than Ben and Thomas had realized, but said he thought it was unlikely they were hiding there since there was no way of reaching it that he could see. (He had not noticed the chimney in the lower cave, and the ascent of the cliff was too perilous.) But Uncle Joseph's eyes were sharper than Old Baldy's. He saw the tiny path that looked, from where he stood, no wider than a cotton thread. Sloping diagonally upwards, it ran round a bluff and disappeared into a gully. It was the sort of path a child would notice, Uncle Joseph thought; it was likely, indeed, that the boys had seen it when they were playing on the beach. It was worth investigating, anyway. He left Old Baldy, watching on the beach, and set off himself on the long walk to the cliff top.

Old Baldy waited. His eyes scanned the empty foreshore, the empty cliff. There was no one in sight. There was no sound except the seagulls and the sound of the sea, chuckling on the beach. He grew bored and yawned until the tears came into his eyes.

Then he saw Ben leave the cave. He watched him until he disappeared round the bluff.

Old Baldy looked grimly at the cliff. He was a cowardly man but he was also a greedy one and it was greed that, in the end, drove him up that dreadful cliff. Uncle Joseph had promised him an enormous reward if he captured Thomas and delivered him up, safe and sound, and Old Baldy did not trust

Uncle Joseph: he was terrified that if Uncle Joseph got to the cave first, and caught Thomas himself, he might be tempted to go back on his promise of the reward. As he climbed, Old Baldy thought of the money he might lose if he didn't hurry. He also sweated with fear that, in his hurry, he might fall. Fear makes people angry and Old Baldy began to be very angry with Thomas. Before he handed the boy over, he would make him pay for this! From time to time, when he stopped to rest, he swore at Thomas under his breath.

By the time he reached the cave, he was in a thoroughly ugly mood. He stood up in the entrance and peered in, blinking. For a moment he could see nothing and rage surged up inside him – had he risked his neck for nothing, after all? Then, right at the back of the cave, in a dark hole in the wall, he saw something move. He bellowed, 'Thomas,' and rushed blindly forward, like a maddened bull.

Thomas did not hear him, of course. Even if he had done, he would not have paid much attention. Because, when he reached the cliff top he had blundered, as Ben had done a few minutes earlier, straight into the arms of Uncle Joseph.

20

LIL IS FORGOTTEN

UNCLE JOSEPH smiled. 'What a surprise! You gave me quite a shock, springing over the clifftop!' Still smiling, he shook his head reproachfully. 'What naughty boys you have been!'

He held them both firmly, by their elbows. They stared at him, too stunned to struggle.

His voice was soft, almost purring. 'But now I have found you, we will say no more about it. We will let bygones be bygones. That is an English idiom, isn't it, Ben?' His glance was sharp as a knife but his voice remained gentle. 'You told me a lie when I saw you in London. I do not like people who lie to me.'

Ben gave a convulsive wriggle but Uncle Joseph's hand slid down from his elbow and tightened on his knuckles, grinding the bones of his hand backwards and forwards.

He said, 'Please do not try to get away from me. If you do, I shall have to hurt you and I do not like to hurt people. Not even naughty boys. Are you going to be good boys, instead, and come with me quietly?'

'Where are you going to take us?' Thomas asked. He looked frightened.

Uncle Joseph smiled broadly. Ben thought: *He would be much less frightening if he didn't smile.*

'You will find out,' he said and set off along the cliff at a smart pace, holding the boys tight by the wrists. They had to run to keep up with him.

They came to what Ben always thought of as the 'tame' part of the cliffs, where the land sloped gently down to the promenade and the town. Here, the wild grass ended, the turf was mown to a velvet finish and there were shelters and wooden benches and a car park for visitors. The car park was empty except for a long, sleek car on the far side. A Jaguar. A yellow Jaguar. *Old Baldy's yellow Jag.*

Ben jerked back frantically but Uncle Joseph's fingers closed on his wrist like a handcuff of steel. Ben yelped. Roused by his cry, Thomas kicked Uncle Joseph as hard as he could, behind the knee. Uncle Joseph gasped, released Ben and gave Thomas a clout that sent him sprawling.

Ben ran a few yards and cannoned blindly into a policeman who was walking across the car park towards them.

The policeman caught hold of him. 'Hullo, young feller-

me-lad,' he said cheerfully. Ben looked up into his kind, red
face with an enormous surge of relief which died as the policeman said, 'Not running off again, are you?' He looked up,
still keeping firm hold of Ben, and said to Uncle Joseph, 'So
you've found them, sir. They seem to be giving you a bit of
trouble. Perhaps I'd better lend a hand.'

Uncle Joseph smiled steadily. 'There is no need for that.
Once they are in the car, they will be no trouble.'

'Taking them to the station, sir? I'll have a lift down, if you
don't mind. I've got to hand in my report to the Superintendent.'

Uncle Joseph hesitated. 'As a matter of fact, I was hoping
to drive straight back to London with my nephew. We have
a plane to catch. But if you think it is really necessary ...'

The policeman looked uncertain. 'Well – it *is* usual, sir. The
boys have been reported missing, haven't they? But I'm sure
the Superintendent wouldn't want you to miss your plane.'
He frowned for a minute. 'Tell you what, this young man
won't be coming with you, will he? He's a Henstable boy. If
you like I'll take him down to the station and make your
excuses to the Superintendent.'

Thomas said softly, 'Oh, *Ben.*' He was holding the side of
his face, where Uncle Joseph had hit him, and trying not to
cry.

Ben clutched at the policeman's sleeve. 'Please,' he said, 'oh,
please. Don't let him take Thomas away. He doesn't want to
go. His uncle wants' – he drew a deep breath – 'he wants to
kidnap him. He's a kidnapper. He ...'

A slow smile spread broadly over the policeman's face. 'Is
he now? Well, well ...'

Uncle Joseph said quickly, 'It is a silly game they have been
playing. You know what children are – what starts as play
becomes quite real to them.'

'You don't have to tell me that,' the policeman said. 'I've
three of my own.' He looked at Ben, quite kindly. 'You've

caused everyone a lot of trouble, you know. Time to stop playing now.'

'But I'm not,' Ben cried. 'I'm *not*. Honestly . . .'

He looked helplessly up into the policeman's kind, grinning face. Then he remembered something Lil had said. If the policeman wouldn't believe the truth, perhaps he would believe a lie. He said, 'His uncle's terrible to him. He beats him and knocks him about. He's *cruel* . . .'

'Oh, come now,' the policeman said. He spoke good-humouredly, but his grin was fading. He had seen the vicious blow Uncle Joseph had given Thomas.

Uncle Joseph saw the doubtful look on the policeman's face. He said, 'Of course the boy is lying. But perhaps it would be better if I did come to the station with you and saw the Superintendent. Then if this young man' – he looked long and hard at Ben – 'has any complaints to make, he can make them in the proper quarter.'

The policeman looked relieved. 'Well, if you don't mind, sir.'

He sat in the back of the car with the boys, large knees spread wide apart, large hands on his knees. His solid presence was a comfort. For a moment, the boys felt safe – but only for a moment. Ben realized almost at once that as soon as Uncle Joseph had spoken to the Superintendent, Thomas would be no safer than he had been on the cliff. Even though the policeman had seen Uncle Joseph knock Thomas down, that wasn't proof that Uncle Joseph was cruel to him. Not cruel, anyway, to the point at which the law would have to step in. And they would never believe the truth: that Uncle Joseph was a kidnapper. Ben could say what he liked, but who would believe him while Uncle Joseph was there, smiling and smiling and talking in that gentle, reasonable voice?

Ben was suddenly nearer to despair than he had ever been in his life.

They got to the station. Uncle Joseph and the policeman

spoke to the sergeant at the desk. The sergeant listened atten-
tively, then he said, 'The Superintendent would like a word
with you, sir. If you would just wait . . .'

He showed them into a side room. He was a large, fierce-
looking man with red, wiry hair sprouting from his nostrils,
but he spoke in a friendly voice.

'They look a miserable pair, don't they, sir? More like a
couple of escaped criminals than two boys who've been res-
cued.' He winked cheerfully at Ben. 'Cheer up for Chatham,
Dover's in sight.'

The boys did not smile. But Uncle Joseph did. 'I think I
have something to cheer my nephew, anyway.' He fumbled
in his pocket. 'I am not really sure that he deserves the present
I have brought for him. But I cannot bear to see a child look
so unhappy.'

'No, indeed,' the sergeant said in a sentimental voice.

Uncle Joseph handed Thomas a small box. Inside, was
a minute and beautiful transistor radio in a red leather
case.

'It is a camera as well. Made in Japan,' Uncle Joseph said.
'It is a very delicate instrument, so you must be very careful,
Thomas, dear.'

He smiled as if there was nothing on his mind except the
desire to give his young nephew pleasure. The sergeant beamed
approvingly, and said, before he left the room, 'He's a very
lucky boy to have such a good uncle. I'm sure the Super won't
keep you a minute, sir.'

In spite of their predicament, both boys were completely
diverted by the marvellous, small machine. They turned it
over, exclaiming.

'It's smashing,' Ben said. 'Really smashing. Look – it's got
an ear-piece, too.'

Thomas turned the radio on. The announcer was reading the
news.

'Get another station,' Ben said. 'We don't want the old news.'

'No,' Thomas whispered. 'Listen . . .'

'. . . *now, a fresh revolution in Tiga. Reports have been coming in from our African correspondent who says it now appears that the attempt to overthrow the present Government has been completely successful. The anti-revolutionary forces, led by Tuku, the brother of the deposed Prime Minister, have occupied the Government buildings and are believed to have captured General Nogola. Prime Minister Okapi is now . . .*'

'Turn it off,' Uncle Joseph said.

He took two swift strides across the room, snatched the radio from Thomas's hand and hurled it to the floor.

Thomas looked at his uncle, and, for a long moment, his uncle looked at him.

He wasn't smiling now.

He said, in a low, even voice that held so much controlled, cold anger that the boys drew instinctively together, 'This is your doing, Thomas. Your fault. You have lost me precious time. If you had not run away, if you had come with me as I wished, my plan would have succeeded. Nogola would still be in power. *I* would be in power.' Suddenly, his control broke. His eyes flashed and he struck himself in the chest with his clenched fist. At that moment, he looked terrible, as terrible as Uncle Tuku. 'I and my family,' he shouted. 'We are the rightful rulers of Tiga. Not your father. Who is your father? A nobody. And Tuku? A nobody, also. And a traitor . . .'

'It's you who is the traitor, by all accounts,' someone said from the door.

Uncle Joseph swung round. Aunt Mabel was standing there, her old tweed coat with the moth-eaten beaver collar, draped round her shoulders. Her long nose was shiny and very red. Her eyes were angry – as angry as Uncle Joseph's. 'I've heard all about you,' she said. 'My brother-in-law's been on the 'phone to me. I didn't like what I heard, I can tell you . . .'

Uncle Joseph marched up to her, his fists clenched. For an awful moment it seemed as if he were going to strike her. But Aunt Mabel out-stared him, contemptuously. He muttered something under his breath, pushed her aside roughly and left the room.

'What manners!' Aunt Mabel said. Then she looked across the room at Ben, and her voice changed. 'Ben,' she cried, and flew at him, arms outspread: she looked like a big, untidy bird. Between kisses, she said breathlessly, 'Ben, Ben, oh, you naughty boy, oh, my darling, never do such a thing again. Oh – I was never so glad to see anyone in my whole life.' She held him away from her and looked searchingly into his face as if to make sure it was really him. 'Oh, Ben – when I found your red jersey I . . .' The tears welled up into her eyes, her nose became redder still and she fell to hugging and kissing him so violently that he began to fear he would smother.

He said, fighting for breath, 'Aunt Mabel. *Aunt Mabel*. This is my friend, Thomas. His mother's in America.'

'I know,' Aunt Mabel said. 'But his father's in England and out of his mind with worry. He's with your father, Ben. They're together, in London. They've been searching up hill and down dale. And all the telephone lines were down – they didn't manage to get through to me until half an hour ago . . .'

Thomas interrupted her. 'Does my father know Uncle Joseph has betrayed him?'

Aunt Mabel nodded. 'He had a message from his brother in Africa. There's been a bit of trouble there, where he comes from . . .'

'A bit of trouble!' Ben burst out indignantly. 'There's been a *revolution*, Aunt Mabel, a bloody revolution . . .'

'Don't use that word, dear. It isn't nice.' She smiled at Thomas. 'Anyway, apparently your naughty Uncle Joseph was at the bottom of it.'

'He wanted to be a great Chief again,' Thomas said wonderingly. 'He betrayed my father. Oh, Ben' – his voice broke – 'I cannot believe it. He is my uncle . . .'

'He is your father's enemy,' Ben said. 'He wanted to capture you so that your father would have to go back to Tiga. And if he had gone back, Nogola would have had him shot as a traitor.'

'That's enough of that sort of talk,' Aunt Mabel said hastily. 'It's all over now. Really – boys of your age shouldn't know about dreadful things like that.'

She spoke, Ben thought, as if they were both about five years old and had been watching something unsuitable on television. Unlike Uncle Tuku, who had treated Thomas as if he were almost a man, Aunt Mabel always behaved as if children were much younger than they were. This had irritated Ben in the past but now, for some reason, he found it curiously comforting. He snuggled close as she sat down, holding both boys firmly within the circle of her bony arms.

'*Now,*' she said. 'I want to know just what you've been doing with yourselves.'

'We hid on the beach.'

'We slept in the cave.'

'I got in and borrowed John's camping things and the ham . . .'

'*Borrowed?*'

'Well, sort of. I mean . . .'

'It was a lovely ham,' Thomas said with a broad, beautiful grin, and Aunt Mabel drew him close and said softly, 'Was it, my lamb? Well – you're welcome to it, then, bless your woolly hair. Did you have anything else to eat?'

'Cockles. But they were nasty. Mostly ham. We had ham for supper and ham for breakfast. We haven't had any lunch. I'm hungry, Aunt Mabel.'

'I daresay I can find you some dry bread and water,' Aunt Mabel said, and smiled.

At that moment, the sergeant opened the door. He said, to Thomas, 'D'you know where your uncle's gone, young man? Funny thing is – he came out a while ago and I told him the Super-'ud see him in a minute but he didn't take a blind bit of notice. Just marched straight out and got into the car and drove off as if the devil was after him.'

'I don't know where he has gone,' Thomas said. 'But I think he was in a hurry.'

'He had a plane to catch,' Ben added and both boys suddenly burst out into such a prolonged roar of helpless laughter that the sergeant looked at Aunt Mabel and put one finger significantly to his forehead before he went out again and shut the door.

When he recovered himself, Ben said, 'Can Thomas come home with us? Are John and Mary out of quarantine?'

'Not quite. But they've promised to stay upstairs and keep out of the way. We're going to look after Thomas until his father comes to fetch him. That may not be just yet – he's very busy with this old revolution. But if he can't come himself, I daresay he'll send someone else quite soon. Perhaps the bald gentleman who was here this morning . . .'

'*Old Baldy*,' said Ben.

They had forgotten Old Baldy. They had forgotten someone else, too.

'Lil,' Ben cried. 'We forgot Lil.'

'Lil?' Aunt Mabel said, but neither of them so much as looked at her.

They were looking at each other. The same fear was dawning in both their minds. It was Thomas who gave voice to it.

'Oh, Ben,' he whispered. 'Suppose – suppose Old Baldy's got her!'

21

THE HOMECOMING

But Lil was safe from Old Baldy. His maddened rush into
the cave had been his undoing. He had blundered blindly
forward and fallen head first down the chimney.

Lil, feeling sleepy and sick, had barely noticed. She had
heard him shout, but only with the edge of her mind: it was
as if someone had shouted in a dream.

It wasn't until some thirty minutes later – about the time Ben
and Thomas arrived at the police station – that she heard him
groan. Her sickness had passed and she woke up fully. She
crawled out of the passage and peered down the chimney but
she could see nothing. She waited a little while, until the
groaning stopped and Old Baldy dragged himself to his feet
and staggered out on to the beach.

He was a sad sight. There was a lump as big as a potato on
one side of his bald skull and one arm hung useless and broken
at his side. He was in great pain. He lurched and tottered along
the beach, stumbling on the shingle. Once, he lost his sense of
direction and wandered aimlessly towards the sea until he fell,
face downwards, in the evil-smelling mud. By the time he
reached the end of the promenade, where the yellow car
was waiting for him, he was filthy, bleeding, and stinking
like a dead fish. He climbed painfully into the passenger
seat and sat there, moaning, while Uncle Joseph ground
the big car into bottom gear and drove angrily out of the
town.

He drove straight to London Airport and took a plane for
Cairo. Where Old Baldy went, no one knew: his name was
not on any passenger list. It seemed, at first, that he had disappeared altogether, but six months later, his aunt received a

coloured postcard. It was a picture of a coffee plantation in Brazil, but it had been posted in Mexico. On the back, Old Baldy had written, Lots of Love, Auntie Dear.

It was the last anyone ever heard of him.

Lil had watched Old Baldy's drunken progress from the mouth of the cave. She was curious rather than frightened. When he was out of sight, she took Joey, climbed to the top of the cliff and walked down to the town. She reached it just as the police car, carrying Aunt Mabel and the two boys, purred up to the cliff top to look for her.

By the time they gave up the search, both boys were in despair. Thomas was weeping softly and Ben was white-faced and full of self-reproaches. They took no notice of Aunt Mabel's attempts to comfort them – and her attempts were not very convincing. Once she had heard about Lil, about her poor mother and the flight from the Welfare Officer, Aunt Mabel was deeply disturbed. Even when Ben told her how smart Lil was in spite of never having been to school, all she said was, 'Poor child – oh, the poor child!'

All three gazed unhappily out of the windows as the police car drove them home.

Thomas said, with a sob, 'I meant to get her some water. She was so thirsty . . .'

Ben said, half to himself, 'We forgot her. It's awful to think we forgot her.'

He rubbed his smarting eyes with the back of his hand and thought that he would never, ever, forgive himself.

The car stopped outside The Haven and Aunt Mabel said, in a strange voice, 'Would *that* be Lil?'

It was. She was sitting on the front steps, Joey's cage on the pavement beside her. Her head was resting against the iron railings and her eyes were half closed.

Aunt Mabel was out of the car and had gone to her before

the boys had time to move. Lil looked up at her and then, slowly, got to her feet. She looked pale and bedraggled but she spoke with dignity.

'I 'spect you don't know who I am. I'm Lil Bates an' I come to look for Ben.'

It was too late for lunch. They would have to make do with high tea, Aunt Mabel said. So they had smoked Finnan haddock and butter and one of Aunt Mabel's best apple tarts with cinnamon and cream. They drank several pints of milk and ate a whole white loaf and the best part of a brown one.

Then they had a great slab of crumbly Wensleydale cheese and a heap of crisp, white celery, followed by apples and yellow Conference pears.

'Sure you've had enough?' Aunt Mabel said. 'I mean, if you haven't, there's the week-end joint. Shall I just pop it into the oven? I would hate to think you were hungry.'

Thomas and Ben were so fuddled with food that they did not realize she was joking. Thomas thanked her politely and said he was very sorry, but he could not eat another crumb. Ben just shook his head.

'What about you, Lil? Is there anything you'd like?'

Aunt Mabel wasn't joking now. All the time Thomas and Ben had been eating – and talking with their mouths full – Lil had sat silently at the table, slowly drinking three cups of strong, sweet tea. She had left untouched the creamy glass of milk Aunt Mabel had first set beside her, as she had left the haddock and the apple pie.

'I expect her stomach's shrunk,' Ben said. 'I mean, we've only been starving for two days but she's been starving for *weeks*. I expect she's done what you always say Mary'll do if she goes on an old slimming diet. Damaged her insides for ever.'

'Be quiet, Ben,' Aunt Mabel said sharply. 'Why don't

you run along and see Miss Pin? She's been asking for you.'

Ben got cautiously down from the table. His stomach felt enormous, like a great, heavy bag. 'I couldn't *run*. I'm too full. I think I'll take Thomas with me. Miss Pin will be interested to see him. She has never seen a black person before.'

He was walking slowly towards the door when, suddenly, he stopped. He stood quite still for a minute. Aunt Mabel saw that his ears and the back of his neck had gone a bright red. He turned and looked at her miserably. 'I haven't got Pin,' he said.

'*Ben*. You've lost him!' Aunt Mabel tossed her head indignantly. 'I told you you'd lose him one day.'

Ben said in a small voice, 'I didn't lose him. I sold him. I *had* to.'

He explained about the pawn shop and Aunt Mabel listened. The expression of righteous annoyance faded from her face and was replaced by a much gentler expression. 'Oh, Ben, I'm so sorry.' She looked at him helplessly. 'So *sorry*.'

His lip quivered. 'It was in a good cause, Aunt Mabel,' he said.

And he went out, sadly and sorrowfully, and closed the door.

Lil said suddenly, 'The pawn shop's in Parker Street.'

It was the first time she had spoken since she came into the house and she looked alarmed, as if the sound of her own voice had scared her.

'Is it? How clever of you to remember,' Aunt Mabel said. Usually she spoke to children in a brisk, rather abrupt way, but to Lil, her manner was different. Her voice was soft and coaxing. 'Come and sit by the fire. You'll be more comfortable.'

Obediently, Lil came to sit where Aunt Mabel had indicated, in a sagging armchair by the open front of the ancient boiler. She sat, still as a pale little statue, staring into the glowing coals, and Aunt Mabel's heart ached for her as it had done from the beginning. Though she longed to take the child in her arms and comfort her, she guessed it would not do: Lil was far too stiff and prickly a person to accept embraces from a stranger. It would be rather like trying to cuddle a hedgehog, Aunt Mabel thought. She drew up her chair and sat opposite Lil, sipping her tea.

After a little, she glanced at Joey who was singing away merrily in his cage on the dresser and said, 'That's a nice budgie. What's his name?'

'Joey,' Lil said, so low that Aunt Mabel could barely hear her.

'He's a pretty bird, isn't he?'

Lil nodded. She looked cautiously at Aunt Mabel. 'Mum says he's company. I don't think birds is much company really.'

'Not as much company as people, I suppose. It must have been a bit lonely in the flat, after your mother went to hospital.'

Lil wriggled her shoulders. 'I don't mind bein' on me own. I c'n look after myself an' . . .'

'I'm sure you can,' Aunt Mabel said. 'I just thought it would be nice if you could stay here with Ben for a bit, until your mother's better.'

Lil shook her head and said nothing.

'It would be quite fun, really,' Aunt Mabel said. 'Henstable's not a bad place. There's the sea and the beach . . .'

'I can't,' Lil said sullenly.

'Why not? Ben and I would like it very much.'

Lil was silent for a minute, then she said in a cross voice, 'This is a boarding house, ain't it? I mean you take in lodgers.'

'In the summer.'

'Well, I can't pay nuthin. An' my Mum says – she says you shouldn't be beholden to nobody.' She sat up straight in the sagging chair and glared at Aunt Mabel defiantly.

Aunt Mabel said mildly, 'Well, you can work for your keep, if you like. You can help me.' She was not usually so tactful but she could see that Lil was just as proud and stiff-necked a person as she was herself and so she knew how she was feeling. And as she also knew that Lil would hate to think anyone was sorry for her, she smiled brightly and added, 'There's a lot to do about a place. You can help me wash the dishes and things like that.'

Lil looked slightly less sour and suspicious. 'All right,' she said grudgingly. 'I don't mind staying if I c'n oblige you a bit.'

'That's settled, then.' Aunt Mabel stood up and riddled the boiler fiercely. The coals sank with a hiss. Then she straightened and said, in casual voice, 'Do you know the name of the hospital where your mother is?'

Lil said, 'There ain't no call to go worryin' her about me.'

'I wouldn't dream of worrying her,' Aunt Mabel said. 'I just thought it would be nice if you could send her a postcard to cheer her up.'

Lil's lip trembled. 'I dunno where she is. They jus' took her off an . . .' Suddenly she crouched forward in her chair as if she had a pain in her stomach and began to cry.

Aunt Mabel watched her for a minute uncertainly. Then she muttered something under her breath and swept Lil off the chair and on to her lap. Lil didn't protest. She just lay, limp as a rag, weeping with exhaustion and a kind of relief while Aunt Mabel rocked her backwards and forwards and crooned, 'There, there, there my lamb . . .'

She was asleep in five minutes. She didn't wake while Aunt Mabel carried her upstairs and gently removed her jeans and jersey and tucked her into bed.

She slept the night through. She didn't wake, even when the wind got up and howled round the house, making a terrible, booming, foghorn noise in the chimneys. She didn't hear the boys go to bed nor their hushed giggling as, a little later, they crept into Mary's room and then into John's. Luckily for them, Aunt Mabel didn't hear the giggling either. She was busy downstairs, making a great many telephone calls.

22

'AFRICA'S AN AWFUL LONG WAY FROM HENSTABLE'

'You were talking on the telephone an awful long time last night, Aunt Mabel,' Ben said at breakfast.

It was a very late breakfast: they had slept until after eleven o'clock and now, at midday, were sitting comfortably down to enormous platefuls of porridge and treacle and yellow, wrinkled cream. Aunt Mabel made very good porridge that was smooth and nutty at the same time and even Lil had consented to try a small bowl of it. Her long sleep – and the terrible ordeal of having a bath and her hair brushed when she woke up – had made her quite hungry.

Aunt Mabel looked at Ben suspiciously. 'How do you know about that? You were in bed. When I looked in, you were sleeping like logs.'

Ben went rather pink and Thomas gave a little, choked giggle that he turned into a cough when Aunt Mabel's eye fell upon him. Of course they had not been asleep when Aunt Mabel had looked in on them but in John's room, sitting on his bed. What Aunt Mabel had seen in their beds had not been boys – or even logs – but two humped-up bolsters and two small, dark cushions they had cunningly placed on their pillows to look like their sleeping heads.

Aunt Mabel's mouth pursed up disapprovingly. 'I do believe . . .' she began.

Ben decided that attack was the best means of defence. He said indignantly. 'We *were* asleep – till you started making all those telephone calls. Ping, ping, ping, on and on. It woke us up and what with that and the wind, we didn't get to sleep again for simply *ages*. Who were you telephoning, Aunt Mabel?'

'Never you mind.' Suddenly, Aunt Mabel smiled. She had spent a second, rather wakeful night; she looked thin as a needle and pale as a wraith, but her smile was mysteriously cheerful. 'Eat up your breakfasts now,' she said, 'or you'll have no appetite for lunch. And we've got roast chicken and . . .'

She stopped. The boys looked up. A car had stopped outside The Haven. Through the open window of the basement kitchen, Ben recognized the uneven throb of the old station taxi.

'*Visitors*,' he said. His heart sank. He loathed the summer visitors: they monopolized the television, ate all the best of the food and took up all Aunt Mabel's time. 'I thought it was the end of the season,' he said in a hollow voice.

'Not ordinary visitors,' Aunt Mabel said. Her face was one broad, beaming smile. 'It's your father, Ben. And Thomas's father, too.'

The boys stared. 'Go on,' Aunt Mabel said. 'Or don't you want to see them?'

The boys fell off their chairs and rushed out of the room and up the basement stairs. Their feet thudded overhead like gunfire; Aunt Mabel looked up with a resigned expression as small, snowy flakes of plaster showered down from the kitchen ceiling. Then she looked at Lil, who was still sitting at the table, staring at her porridge plate.

'Aren't you going too?' Aunt Mabel said.

Lil looked up, poker-faced. 'Do I have to?'

Aunt Mabel just smiled. 'Come here,' she said.

181

Lil hesitated. Then she slipped off her chair and went over to Aunt Mabel who scrubbed at her mouth with a corner of her apron, looked at the result critically, gave another dab with the apron and tweaked at the clean ribbon she had tied in her hair. 'You'll do,' she said, and started up the stairs.

Lil followed her, but only because Aunt Mabel so clearly expected it. For herself, she would have preferred to stay in the kitchen. She was glad, for her friends' sake, that Mr Mallory and Chief Okapi had come, but no one had come for her and it made her feel lonely and miserable.

The sun was streaming through the open front door into the narrow hall. Outside on the pavement, Thomas was embracing a tall, black man. He was almost as large as Uncle Tuku and he wore the same kind of splendid robes. Ben was standing by the open door of the taxi smiling up at his father and his father's arm was round his shoulders in such a gentle, loving way that it brought a small, hard lump into Lil's throat. They all looked so happy. Lil felt she could not endure their happiness. She wanted to creep away somewhere and cry quietly, by herself.

Aunt Mabel took her hand and squeezed it tight as if she guessed what Lil was feeling. She whispered, 'Wait a minute, pet. Just a minute.'

Lil saw that Mr Mallory had taken his arm from Ben's shoulders and was leaning forward into the taxi, both hands outstretched. He was helping someone out, someone who must be either very old, or very infirm. Two thin hands emerged and gripped at his arms and then, slowly, a thin, pale, young woman stepped down and stood unsteadily on the pavement.

Beside Aunt Mabel, Lil began to tremble like a leaf.

Aunt Mabel said gently, 'I tried about every hospital in London . . .'

Lil opened her mouth, but no sound came out.

'What's the matter? Cat got your tongue?' Aunt Mabel

said, and gave her a little push, between the shoulder blades. Lil looked like a child in a dream. She took a few, faltering paces, then stopped. Stopped and stared . . .

Then, suddenly, the spell that held her seemed to break, and she rushed forward.

'Mum,' she shouted, with such joy that it sounded almost like a cry of anguish. 'My Mum, oh, my Mum, my Mum.' Her voice was so piercing that passers-by turned to stare as she flew down the steps and across the pavement. Mr Mallory put out a hand to stop her, afraid she would thud into Mrs Bates and knock her over, but Lil checked her exuberant rush of her own accord. She came to a skidding halt and looked up into her mother's face. She held her breath. The pale young woman bent, with tears in her eyes, and, very gently, Lil put up her rough little hands and stroked the thin cheeks. 'Oh, Mum,' she whispered. 'I took good care of Joey, just like you said.'

The chicken they had for lunch was beautiful, surrounded by crisp curls of bacon and roasted as it should be, with the brown skin crackly yet full of juice. But no one really noticed how good it was except Thomas, perhaps, and Ben, certainly. There were few circumstances in which Ben could not appreciate good food.

Lil and her mother were engrossed in each other. They sat with their chairs drawn close together, not talking, only looking and touching and occasionally exchanging bright, private smiles. From time to time, one of them would furtively slip an especially choice morsel on to the other's plate, but neither ate very much, for all that.

Nor did Aunt Mabel. She was hypnotized by Chief Okapi who sat at the head of the table, magnificent in his blue and scarlet blanket. His naked shoulder gleamed like brown satin; he wore gold rings in his ears. No one so exotic and extra-ordinary had ever come into Aunt Mabel's boarding house before. She was so taken up with him that she did not even notice when Ben ran his forefinger round his empty plate to trap the last of the delicious juice.

In the end, Mr Mallory had to speak quite loudly to attract her attention. 'Mabel. *Mabel*. I think Mrs Bates is feeling a little tired . . .'

At once, Aunt Mabel was all solicitude. 'How dreadful of me – I'm so sorry. Of course, you must have a nice rest . . .'

'It's all right, really. I don't want to be a nuisance,' Mrs Bates murmured.

'You aren't. Ben – come and help me get Mrs Bates up-stairs.'

'*I* c'n help my Mum,' Lil said and was off her chair and had put her small arms round her mother before Ben had time to move. She glared round the table as if daring anyone else to touch her.

'You're not strong enough, dear,' Mr Mallory said. This was a very foolish thing to say to Lil, but then he did not know her very well.

Lil went bright pink. 'I am, I *am*. I'm terribly strong for my age,' she said passionately.

'Please let her,' Mrs Bates said. Though she was indeed very tired, she managed to smile up at Mr Mallory. She had a pretty smile, she would be a pretty woman, Mr Mallory thought, if she did not look so wretchedly ill. She stood up shakily, leaning heavily on Aunt Mabel on one side and lightly – very lightly – on Lil's bony little shoulder on the other.

When they had left the dining-room and were going slowly up the stairs, Ben said, 'Dad – is Lil's Mum very ill?'

'Not ill, exactly. But they didn't really want her to leave the hospital. Her legs are all right now – they weren't badly broken and she just needs exercises now – but the doctor said she's still very weak. He says she was under-nourished – half starved – when she came into the hospital.'

'Lil's Dad has left them,' Ben said. 'So I expect they didn't have any money to buy food.' He paused. 'Lil says her Dad is nice, but I don't think he can be. Do you?'

Mr Mallory looked at his son. 'I wouldn't presume to say. Mrs Bates has had *some* money, though perhaps not enough. She had a part-time job in a shop. But I'm afraid she won't be able to go back to that, just yet. So I really don't know . . .'

Mr Mallory didn't have time to tell them what he didn't know because, at that moment, Aunt Mabel called to him. He went out into the hall and saw her leaning over the banisters. Her long nose was red as it usually was when she was excited or upset about something.

'Come up here,' she said. 'Come and tell that poor soul she must stay here as long as she likes. She's all set to go back to London as soon as she's had a bit of a rest and take the child with her. It's absurd! She's not fit!'

Mr Mallory knew she was right. But he was not sure it would be easy to convince Mrs Bates of it, nor that Aunt Mabel was the right person to do so. She had a good heart but rather a high-handed manner. Her tactful behaviour to Lil had been really quite exceptional. Usually, when she thought she knew what was good for people, she told them what it was straight out, and expected them to agree with her.

Mr Mallory went into the best spare bedroom, where Mrs Bates was lying on the bed, under the eiderdown. Her face was almost as white as the pillows, but her eyes were bright and defiant. So were Lil's. She was sitting beside her mother and holding her hand. When Mr Mallory and Aunt Mabel came in, she got up and stood protectively between them and the bed.

Mrs Bates said, 'Mr Mallory, you've all bin very kind. But I – I can't let you – I mean I can't stay here. I'll be a bit stronger, by an' by, and then we'll be able to git back to London.'

Mr Mallory said nothing. He walked round to the other side

of the bed, pulled up a chair and sat down. He smiled at Mrs Bates for a minute and then he said thoughtfully, 'You know, I think Lil could do with a bit of sea air. She looks pale to me.'

'I'm *not* pale,' Lil said. 'If I am, it's jus' 'cause I'm *naturally* pale. It's jus' the colour my skin is *naturally*.'

'Thin, too,' Mr Mallory said. 'She could do with a bit of feeding up. And, you know, there's nothing would please my sister-in-law more. She's an excellent cook, even though she may be a bit bossy.'

He grinned at Aunt Mabel's indignant look.

Mrs Bates did not answer. She was staring at Lil who did indeed look thin – scarecrow thin, a famine child. She said, under her breath, 'They tol' me at the hospital she was all right. They said she was bein' looked after.'

'She was,' Mr Mallory said. 'Ben looked after her.'

Mrs Bates turned her head slowly on the pillows and looked at him. 'She won't stay without me.'

'I know that,' Mr Mallory said.

Mrs Bates's mouth shook a little. 'I don't want to be beholden to anyone.'

Aunt Mabel smiled grimly.

Mr Mallory said quietly, 'We're all beholden to each other, in a sort of way,' and suddenly Mrs Bates closed her eyes and the slow tears squeezed out from under her lids.

Almost imperceptibly, she nodded her head.

'That's settled then,' Mr Mallory said. He got up quickly before Mrs Bates could say thank you. He had the feeling that, like Aunt Mabel, she was one of those people to whom saying 'thank you' did not come easily. He patted Lil on the head as he passed her, and said, 'Keep your Mum company, there's a good lassie.'

'I'll sing 'er to sleep,' Lil said. 'She likes me to sing when she's tired. She likes hymns best.'

She sat on the edge of the bed and sang:

'A few more years shall roll,
A few more seasons come,
And we shall be with those that are
Asleep within the tomb . . .'

'A rather gloomy choice for a lullaby,' Mr Mallory said, as he closed the door.

'She's a good child,' Aunt Mabel said unexpectedly – it was unlike her to praise anyone. Then she added, 'Have you got it?'

Mr Mallory seemed to know what she meant. 'Yes. I had to pay through the nose, though.'

'It doesn't matter what it cost, as long as you got it.'

Mr Mallory raised his eyebrows. 'That's not like you, Mabel.'

'There are times when money's important and times when it isn't,' she said. She looked at her brother-in-law. 'He's a fine man, Chief Okapi. Sat at the table and ate his chicken just like anyone else.'

'What did you expect, Mabel?' Mr Mallory asked curiously.

'I really don't know,' she said in a surprised voice and stuck her long, pink nose in the air.

While they were upstairs, Chief Okapi was talking to the boys in the dining-room. They both leaned against his great knees and looked up into his face, which was extremely kind and gentle.

He was a gentle, kind man, and a very trusting one too, which was probably why he had never guessed that Uncle Joseph was really his enemy. Though Uncle Joseph was clever and cunning, a more suspicious man than Chief Okapi might have seen through him long ago. But Chief Okapi had trusted Uncle Joseph and loved him as a brother and he spoke of him now with grief, not anger. 'He is his own worst enemy,' he said sadly. 'He has exiled himself from his home for ever. He will never dare to come to Tiga again.'

Much of what he told the boys they knew – or had guessed

– but there were some things they did not know or had not altogether understood. Uncle Joseph had always wanted power for himself. He had bribed General Nogola to seize power for him in return for the revenue from the diamond mines, and he had planned to take over the country when the revolution was complete and Chief Okapi either dead, or imprisoned. When Chief Okapi fled the country, Uncle Joseph knew that his plan had failed and that he must come to England and bide his time. At first he had thought he need do nothing except wait: it had looked, in the beginning, as if the British Government would do what Nogola had asked, and send Chief Okapi back to Tiga. When they had released him instead, he had decided to kidnap Thomas, to return with him to Tiga and force his father to return as well.

'But even if he had taken me back, you need not have followed me,' Thomas said. 'I would have been all right. Uncle Joseph is a bad man, but he would never have hurt me.'

His father shook his head sadly. 'Not himself. He would not have wished to have his nephew's blood on his hands. But he would have handed you over to Nogola, as he would have done with me . . .'

He turned, to look gravely at Ben. 'So you see,' he said, 'I have to thank you, not only for my country, but also for my son.'

Ben swelled with pride. He wished his father and Aunt Mabel were here, to hear this.

Chief Okapi said, 'Before we go home to Tiga, Thomas and I, I would like . . .'

'But you're not taking Thomas away yet,' Ben burst out. 'Oh, please – not yet.'

'We shall have to leave tomorrow,' Chief Okapi said gently. 'I am very sorry, Ben. But, before we go, I would like to give you a present.'

Ben turned very red. 'I don't want a *present*,' he said in a rude, loud voice.

Chief Okapi smiled. 'It is the custom in my country to give presents to people who have helped you. It is not an insult.'

'Oh. I see. I'm sorry.' Ben swallowed. What he wanted – *all* he wanted – was for Thomas to stay a little longer but he knew this was impossible. 'There's nothing I want really,' he said absently, thinking how dull everything was going to be once Thomas had gone. Then his heart gave a jump. There *was* something. He only had a pound left of the thirty shillings he had got for Pin. 'Perhaps I could have ten shillings,' he said.

Chief Okapi looked surprised. Aunt Mabel, who came in at that moment with Mr Mallory, looked angry. '*Ben*,' she said. 'Really, Ben! You must never ask people for money.'

Behind her, Mr Mallory laughed. 'It's not money he wants, Mabel. It's this. Isn't it, Ben?'

He took something out of his pocket and held it up between his finger and thumb.

Ben stared. He could not speak. It was Thomas who said, 'Oh, *Ben*. It's Pin come back . . .'

Ben gasped. He rushed to his father and took the little horse from his hand. He stroked Pin lovingly, feeling the dear, familiar shape, the delicate legs, the tiny ears. His face glowed as he looked up at his father and said, 'How ever did you find him, Dad?'

'Lil told Mabel where the pawn shop was and Mabel told me.' Mr Mallory grinned. 'Dared me to come down without it.'

'Fancy Lil remembering!' Ben thought about Lil for a minute, then he said slowly, 'If I mayn't ask for money for myself, could I ask for some for Lil? Just a little, to help out till her Mum's better.' He sighed. 'I don't suppose she'd take it, though. She's awfully stuck-up and snooty.'

Chief Okapi's eyes twinkled. 'I expect your father can think of some way to arrange it tactfully. If that is what you wish,

Ben, I will be pleased to help Lil and her mother. But is there nothing you would like for yourself? Something to help you to remember your good friend Thomas, once he has gone?'

'I shan't need helping,' Ben said. 'I – I shall remember Thomas for ever and ever.' He looked at Thomas and Thomas looked at him, his eyes solemn and sad. Ben felt very sad too – and helpless. Thomas was his friend, they had had a splendid adventure together, but now it was over and Thomas was going away and there was nothing Ben could do to stop his going. They might not meet again for years and years – not until they were both old. And perhaps, by then, they would have forgotten each other, after all.

'Africa's an awful long way from Henstable,' Ben said, half to himself.

Thomas's eyes filled with tears.

Chief Okapi laughed. 'Not so very far. The world is becoming a small place, Ben.' He looked at Mr Mallory. 'If your father would allow it, there is nothing to prevent your visiting Thomas, if you wish. Next year, for your summer holidays, perhaps?'

Ben clutched Pin so tightly that the sharp ears dug into the palm of his hand.

'Well, Ben, what do you say?'

Ben opened his mouth and closed it again. He felt curiously muzzy and light-headed and his ears seemed to be singing. After a long moment, he managed to say in a strangled voice, 'I'd like to. Of course I'd like to. But . . .'

He stopped. It would cost pounds – hundreds of pounds – to fly to Tiga. He could hardly say to Chief Okapi that his father could not afford the fare.

'But what?' Chief Okapi looked at Ben. His eyes were still full of laughter but he inclined solemnly. 'Naturally, from the moment you left your aunt's house, you would be the guest of the Government of Tiga. The honoured guest,' he said.

A HANDFUL OF THIEVES

When the sinister Mr Gribble disappears with Gran's savings, Fred and the other members of the Cemetery Committee decide to take on a dangerous and hair-raising chase to track down the thief and rescue the stolen savings.

THE WHITE HORSE GANG

Sam, Rose and Abe are the White Horse Gang. They hatch a shocking plot to kidnap a little boy – and then find how hard it is to be as ruthless as proper kidnappers.

THE WITCH'S DAUGHTER

All the children were frightened of Perdita, until Tim and his blind sister Janey came from the mainland along with the sinister Mr Jones. This is a fine story about two lonely girls, and it is also an exciting mystery.

THE RUNAWAY SUMMER

Mary is an unpleasant, unlikeable, unhappy girl whose parents are getting a divorce. She is sent to stay with her grandfather and awful Aunt Alice, who live by the sea, and there she meets Simon, the policeman's son. Together they come across an illegal immigrant boy, Krishna, and resolve to outwit the police and find the boy's uncle for him.

THE ROBBERS

Philip has to decide whether to obey his father or to help Doug, his friend – and finds it the most difficult decision he's ever had to make.

SQUIB

'Who said Squib was unhappy?' said Robin. 'You can't go tearing off to the police and say 'Look, there's this kid in the park, we don't know who he is or where he lives or anything about him, but he's shy and he's got odd eyes and a bit of a bruise on one leg.' But Kate simply had to find out about the strange, frightened little boy, and in doing so got into the most terrifying situation of her life.

CARRIE'S WAR

Bombs were falling on London, and Nick and Carrie were evacuated to Wales where they were billeted with Mr Evans, a bit of an ogre, and his timid mouse of a sister. Their friend Albert was luckier, living in Druid's Bottom with Hepzibah Green and the strange Mister Johnny, and Carrie and Nick were happy to visit him there, until Carrie did a terrible thing, the worst thing she ever did in her life.

THE PEPPERMINT PIG

Johnnie was only a little runt, a peppermint pig, which cost Mother a shilling, but somehow his great naughtiness and cleverness kept Poll and Theo cheerful even though it was one of the most difficult years of their lives.

THE SECRET PASSAGE

Life was boring for the three children, living with their disagreeable aunt, after their happy home in Africa, but all is changed with the discovery of the secret passage.

REBEL ON A ROCK

Twelve-year-old Jo, on holiday with her family, stumbles into a revolutionary plot and decides to try and prevent its execution.